# STACKS

Benjamin Lebert

## THE BIRD IS A RAVEN

Benjamin Lebert was born in Freiburg,
West Germany, in 1982.

VINTAGE

**INTERNATIONAL**

# THE BIRD IS A RAVEN

# THE BIRD IS A RAVEN

BENJAMIN LEBERT

*Translated from the German
by Peter Constantine*

*Vintage International*
Vintage Books
A Division of Random House, Inc.
New York

FIRST VINTAGE INTERNATIONAL EDITION, JANUARY 2007

*Translation copyright © 2005 by Peter Constantine*

All rights reserved. Published in the United States by Vintage Books,
a division of Random House, Inc., New York, and in Canada by
Random House of Canada Limited, Toronto. Originally published in German
as *Der Vogel ist ein Rabe* by Verlag Kiepenheuer & Witsch, Köln, in 2003.
Copyright © 2003 by Verlag Kiepenheuer & Witsch.
This translation originally published in hardcover in the United States by
Alfred A. Knopf, a division of Random House, Inc., New York, in 2006.

Vintage is a registered trademark and Vintage International and colophon are
trademarks of Random House, Inc.

Grateful acknowledgment is made to Sailor Music for permission to reprint an
excerpt from "The Joker" by Steven H. Miller, Ahmet Ertegun and Eddie Curtis.
Copyright © 1973 by Sailor Music, Warner-Tamerlane Music, Jim Rooster
Music. All rights reserved. Reprinted by permission of Sailor Music.

The Library of Congress has cataloged the Knopf edition as follows:
Lebert, Benjamin, 1982—.
[Der Vogel ist ein Rabe. English.]
The bird is a raven / Benjamin Lebert ; translated from the original German
by Peter Constantine.
p. cm.
I. Constantine, Peter, 1963– II. Title
PT2672.E28V6413 2005
833'.92—dc22
2005040705

**Vintage ISBN: 978-1-4000-7806-6**

*Book design by Virginia Tan*

www.vintagebooks.com

Printed in the United States of America
10  9  8  7  6  5  4  3  2  1

*For Lillemor Malin Brandt*

# THE BIRD IS A RAVEN

I finished high school in Munich. When I was twenty I moved to Berlin to study ethnology. I shared an apartment in Schöneberg with two other students. A guy named Randall and a girl named Sofia. I hardly spent any time studying. I didn't really give a damn about anything. I hung out in the city. I went to cafés and clubs. I met people who were doing the same thing. Most of them had come to Berlin from somewhere else. In fact, they all had. And they all wanted to be discovered. Of course, they knew that they had to go out looking too. And they did that to some extent. But they wanted above all to be discovered.

It's Friday night, 10:26, January 4. I'm standing on platform 18 of the central station in Munich.

My green duffel bag is lying next to me on the ground. It's bitter cold. The wind is shaving my cheeks. Solitary pigeons are fluttering around; one of them lands on the tracks. The station concourse is brightly lit. There aren't many people around. An elderly woman in a black coat is standing a few yards away from me. She's wearing a white hat with earflaps. She's walking back and forth, her left arm crossed over her chest, her right hand holding a cell phone, whose buttons she's pressing with her thumb. More solitary figures. The train is already six minutes late. It's the train that'll take me back to Berlin after my short visit home. Berlin, where everything is bright and beautiful. At least that's what you used to hear. From everyone. From all the guys who were raving about Berlin: man, you gotta go there. It's a great town. It's like, you know, everything's moving! There's action there. The air isn't air—it's filled with gold dust. You know, like, you inhale gold dust. And the girls! They're incredible! Whether they've been there all along or just arrived, you can tell they've been breathing in tons of gold dust.

But none of that was really true. I mean, the girls I came across in Berlin, most of them were really great, but they weren't breathing gold dust. The air they sucked in through their beautiful noses was nostalgia. And not just the girls.

I stare at the announcement board: 10:29. The train will be here any minute. I think of the three days I've just spent in Munich, think about my mother. She's a doctor. Each night when I sleep at my parents' house, she puts a little white bowl of sliced kiwis on my nightstand. She used to do that before too. Now it gets on my nerves. But in Berlin I still think about it. When I'm at a club and see all the people who have come to the city like me and are dancing like crazy. All of them with this expectant look in their eyes, which can even be detected in the dim lights of the club. Maybe only really detectable in the dark. Like shimmering cats' eyes. And then I wonder if they have somebody somewhere who, regardless of what happens, will keep on putting sliced kiwis on their nightstand.

The loudspeaker announces the train and it pulls in, the wheels grinding. As I get on, I suddenly feel sick, like I'm going to fall backward onto the platform. But I don't. I'm carrying my bag over my shoulder. I squeeze my way though the corridor. Past two girls who only grudgingly make way. One of them is chewing gum. Where's the sleeper? My compartment is number 39. It's a long walk. I also have to go through the dining car. It's quite full. Blue cigarette smoke hangs over the tables. Voices and laughter. Beneath my feet I feel that the train has started up again. At last, number 39.

A white card key is sticking in the door. I unlock it. The second bed is still empty. Mine is the bottom one. Not much space here. On a shelf are two bananas, two apples. There are also two upturned drinking glasses and two little bottles of water. In front of the window: drawn gray curtains with small violet dots. The door to the washroom is narrow. A shower cubicle, a toilet, a small washbowl. Pretty much all the colors in the compartment are gray and violet. It somehow smells of plastic, not of fresh air. Not of air that nine hours later, when we arrive in Berlin, will transform itself into gold dust. I hang my brown coat on a hook, sit down on my bed. Not quite sure if I should undress, or wait till the other guy gets here. I can hear the sounds from the compartment next door quite clearly. A woman's voice says: "I've had enough; I can't go on."

Last time I traveled in a sleeper, there was some old guy in the upper bunk who kept calling down to me that I should come up for a fuck. Back then I wasn't into it. And I'm still not. That's why I'm wondering who'll be coming in this time. There's a knock. I open the door. My sleeper companion turns out to be a young guy, about my age. He's small and delicate-looking, has short brown hair, and a black backpack, which he immediately puts down next to my bag. From his movements, the way he keeps shifting his weight from one foot to the other and darting his head back and forth, I think right away: a bird.

"What's up?" he says.

"Hi there," I say. We smile at each other.

"Want to hit the dining car?"

"Yeah, let's go for it."

I'm not actually hungry, but I think it'll do me good to chat a bit before going to sleep.

A small table frees up in the dining car. What will we drink? He orders an apple juice, I order a beer. It's black outside. You can't see anything of the landscape, except for a few lights. Our faces are mirrored in the windows. The drinks arrive. A small, homey lamp is burning on the table. He also orders fried eggs and spinach.

"I could eat a cow!" he says. "By the way, my name's Henry."

"I'm Paul."

The train takes a curve, the waitress balances her tray past us. Is it the monotonous clack-clack of the wheels creating this peculiar mood? An anonymous familiarity, like two strangers on a hike who meet by a river. They sit down together. They don't know each other. Their only link is the river.

"I'm heading for Berlin," Henry says. "I have no other choice."

His fried eggs arrive. I've never seen anyone scarf down two eggs and spinach faster. He wipes his mouth with his napkin and looks at me. "You've got a brown spot in your eye. In the white part. What's that?"

"My mom noticed it too and brought it up. No idea what that's all about. I've just had it three days."

He sits there for a while as if he were asleep with his eyes open. Just as I am about to ask him when he ate last, he begins talking: "I had two friends. They were my only friends. We stuck together. When I was hanging out with them I wasn't afraid of anything. Their names were Jens and Christine. They were both older than me. Jens was twenty-three and Christine was twenty-eight. I'm eighteen. Now we won't be together anymore. Ever."

For a moment there is silence.

"Do you mind if I smoke?" he asks. He doesn't wait for an answer. He pulls a cigarette from his pack of Marlboros and hands me one too. He lights both. A few lit houses wipe past our windows. Then there's blackness again.

"I don't understand," Henry continues. "I don't understand how it all happened. That's why I have to talk about it with someone. If I talk about it with someone, it'll all come back again and I'll figure it out. Remembering things is so fucking important. Because you have to remember things before you can deal with them. I just have to go over it again and—" He breaks off. "You know what I mean?" he asks after a while.

"Yeah, sure do," I answer, and cautiously add, "It's not all that hard to understand."

"There's nothing to understand," he retorts sharply. Suddenly a fire rages in his eyes. "I mean, I have no idea how she's doing. And I don't know if I'm ever going to see her again. After all that stuff."

The train stops in a brightly lit station. A traveler comes into the dining car, sits down at a table, and orders a cup of coffee. The waitress says, "We're no longer serving." The traveler is angry. She couldn't care less. She comes to our table and says, "I'm closing up now."

I hadn't noticed that the dining car had emptied out.

"Separate checks?"

"No, one check," Henry says, and puts his wallet on the table.

"Seventeen euros, or thirty-four marks."

He hasn't touched his apple juice. We go back to our compartment. We lie down in our bunks. The lights are out. But I've opened the window curtains. Blackness flies past, like an enormous cloud of dark insects. The moving train provides the musical accompaniment. "I hate the darkness," Henry says. "This might sound weird, but for me darkness always sheds light on terrible things." He hesitates for a moment. Then he starts talking.

"I don't know how it is with you, but my biggest problem is girls. I always wanted to be with a girl, but I couldn't get it together. Those school dances were the worst. I'd watch them all dancing. But not with me. Their straps would slip down over their shoulders, and the stupid guys dancing with them would pull them back up with a cheesy grin. I would have done anything to be the guy to pull a girl's strap back up over her shoulder. But it never happened. And the girls all looked so good. Like they were glowing. And they smelled as if just before coming to the party they'd been lying in some magical perfumed meadow in another world, another universe. I was always standing there, so far away from it all. Even though I was so close. The people on the dance floor were inside an invisible bubble. And I was outside. That's a little weird, if you think about it. I could have walked up to one of the girls, you know, to touch her shoulder. But I wouldn't really be touching her shoulder. Just the bubble, right? I also couldn't really dance. At those parties there was only one thing I was good at. The one thing I was always good at: taking a shit. I always got the shits. I'd run to the toilet and shit my brains out. I'd hunch forward, sweating so my clothes stuck to my skin, and I'd have to struggle to yank down my shorts. And with everything that came pouring out, I couldn't shit out my sadness. What's more, I'd be pissed off at the girls. I'd see them there, dancing, giggling like idiots, while those assholes had their arms wrapped around them, squeezing their breasts. I'd be thinking: girls aren't the wonderful creatures I imagined them to be, delicate and sensitive and soft and vulnerable, who always have to be looked after and all that. Girls are jerks. They know exactly what they're doing to you."

I hear the bunk creak above me. And then his voice again: "Christine was the first, the first one I really fell in love with. I'm actually related to her, in a roundabout way. So I've known her from childhood. She lived in Belgium. I'd sometimes see her at family get-togethers, or over the holidays. I remember she always had an attitude with me, and she would lie in the sun with her chin up as if she was balancing something on it. And she'd never play soccer with me in the yard. Unlike her little brother, who I liked a lot more. Until one day she moved in with my grandmother in Munich. She must have been about twenty-six then. And sick. I was living in Munich too, with my mom. Grandmother is my mother's mother. I'd often visit my grandmother. She lived in the suburbs. We went for walks together. She'd tell me stories of days long gone that were now high up in the sky, hidden and invisible among twinkling stars. Days that had to be brought back through her stories. My grandmother was good at that. At bringing back stories from somewhere. When Christine moved in with her, I visited her even more often. Sometimes I slept there. I didn't know what was wrong with Christine. She was very pale, hardly spoke, and had an absent look on her face. As I found out later, that was part of her disease. She didn't have that giggle I couldn't stand in other girls, she always just sat in a chair, her feet bare. Her feet were tiny. I'd watch them. They didn't look like feet you could walk around on. The skin on her soles was completely soft. Like it was everywhere on her body. Christine's body was immaculate. Long thin legs, thin arms, small breasts, her nipples stood out

under her T-shirt. She never wore a bra. Wait, I for-
got to say that her skin had a golden glow. And her
long hair was brown. She slept in a blue bed in the
remodeled attic. I slept on the couch in the living
room whenever I didn't head back home in the
evening. One night—can you imagine?—I went
up the stairs and sat on the top step for five hours.
Just to be near her—can you imagine?"

Henry clears his throat. Suddenly he goes off in
a completely different direction: "So, we're heading to Berlin. Great! Tell me about the city. What's
the deal in Berlin?"

"What?"

"I don't know anything about Berlin. Can you
fill me in?"

"Why?"

"Just to change the subject. Come on, please,
tell me."

I think. I hadn't reckoned that I'd suddenly have
to say something. And I'm really not in the mood. I
notice how hard it is for the words to come out.
"Just to change the subject," I repeat. "Berlin. That
city eats you up. That's what occurs to me off the
cuff. Literally bites off parts of your body. I mean it.
When you walk the streets—like, wherever you

go—you see people lying there left and right, the city having bitten off one of their legs. Or a hand. At some point they're totally devoured. And even if some of them haven't been devoured yet, at least every one of them has been slobbered over. The place is full of people slobbered over by Berlin. And you're one of them. When you walk around, you have the feeling you're on a hike. That's how much your feet hurt. I see the color of the city as gray. And the sky's almost always white. Gross, like a grimy white sheet stretched over the rooftops. A real downer."

"Great," Henry replies. "Great prospect. Your report is so bright and cheerful that I'll give myself up to Berlin the instant I arrive."

"Unfortunately that's the way it is," I say. "For me that's just the way the city is."

"What about the people?"

"What about them?"

"I hear they do all kinds of whacked stuff."

For a few heartbeats there is silence. Then he speaks again. "Well, of course, people do all sorts of whacked stuff—in general, I mean. And they're disgusting and all that. But there's also something heartbreaking about them. They know they're going to die someday. They have no idea what's going to happen to them after that. They don't know if they're alone in the endless universe or if anyone sees them at all and thinks: they sure were brave today. They don't even know if they're destined for something, or if their existence is just an accident, and all that. And still they try to get excited about a cup of tea, you know, or they tell each other stories in a night train. Or during their summer vacation they travel from one corner of the globe — that is so tiny in comparison to the universe — to another corner, where they lie on a beach and try to be happy."

"Yes," I reply. "They sure try. Does the train make you feel good?"

"The train's bringing me to a new place," Henry says, more to himself than to me. And after a few moments he asks: "How long does it take to get slobbered over by Berlin?"

I had gone to Berlin in a truck. In the back: my bed, my clothes, my desk, my CDs. In front, at the wheel: my father. The way he sees it, you've really got to experience the first move of your life. You've got to do it yourself. And he had rented the truck. It was much too big. You could have moved the whole Hellabrunn Zoo with it. Maybe my father just wanted to show that he had a truck license. It was summer. It was hot. I can still see him there, sweat dripping from his forehead.

In two weeks, he told me, he'd be in Berlin and visit me. In two weeks. He's the kind of guy who grabs the bull by the horns. Pliers, drills, squash rackets, New Year's Eve fireworks. He wants to buy me and my roommates a new washing machine. And hook it up for us too.

If something goes wrong in life and he can't do anything about it—like when his younger brother died—he stops rushing around and becomes real still.

Henry says: "Anorexia is a totally weird disease. I didn't know there was such a thing. You just don't eat anything. You get thinner and thinner till you die. That's what Christine had. It started when she was living alone in Brussels. At the beginning it didn't show. She was just one of the many beautiful thin girls. Her parents thought at first that she was just acting up. Because she'd be sitting at the table picking at her food with her fork. When she visited her parents she'd bring along a bottle of soy oil. Something to do with fatty acids. She'd brush some into the pan and fry herself a tiny turkey steak. And then she'd just eat a few bites. Sometimes she'd go to the toilet and spit those few bites out too."

"Why would anyone do a thing like that?" I ask.

Henry says: "It's psychological. And if it's not treated, the people who have it die. I'm serious. Christine was put in a clinic in Bavaria near where my grandma lives. Her parents had moved to some-where near Paris, and had no idea what to do. She was in the clinic for three months. Then she moved to my grandma's. We were the only people she knew in Germany. But she wanted to stay. A few weeks later she showed me the clinic. We went by train—it was a lovely sunny day, Lake Chiem was glittering. The clinic looked nice, like one of those picture-postcard chalets. Geraniums on all the balconies. Terraces, a big garden. We spent the night at a small inn in a double bed. Imagine! Christine and me in a double bed! I don't have to tell you I didn't sleep all night. I counted every breath she took. My whole body felt so heavy that I could hardly breathe. But my heart was breathing. In the morning at breakfast she told me about Jens. Jens had been at the clinic the same time she was. He wasn't anorexic—he was obese. You know the name of that disease? It's called adiposity. That's psychological too. The clinic specialized in people with eating disorders: the really thin and the really fat, and people who look normal and eat normal but stick a finger down their throat after every meal so they can throw up. That's called bulimia, and that's psychological too. Jens lived alone in Munich. Studying political science—already working on his dissertation, Christine told me.

"One day I met Jens in a café in Schwabing. I was floored when I saw him. He was enormous, and enormously fat. He had a round, flattened, friendly face, with a jutting chin, blue eyes, and cropped blond hair. According to him he had already lost fifty pounds at the clinic. He'd been a lot fatter. I liked him right away. The three of us were supposed to meet there, but Christine hadn't shown up yet. Jens carefully made his way over to my table and asked in a raspy, high-pitched voice: 'Are you Henry?'

"I nodded. He was wearing an open light-brown

leather jacket and a red-and-blue checked shirt over his faded XXL jeans. We smiled at each other. He took off his jacket, hung it on the back of his chair, and sat down.

"'I knew you'd be late again, baby face!' he said to Christine when she turned up. The two of them always called each other 'baby face,' 'honey bunch,' 'sweetness.' At first because they wanted to make fun of the awful people who used such ridiculous expressions. But then it became routine. Soon you couldn't tell if they were making fun or not. Regardless of how fucked up they felt, they swam in a lagoon of baby-face honey-bunch sweetness. And that was as bad as when others swam in it. If not worse. And I asked myself what they saw in each other. He was fat, she was thin. He was almost six foot four, she was tiny. Everyone turned to look at her because she was so pretty, and at him too—though not because he was so pretty. And nothing pointed to what a catastrophic trio we were going to become."

I hear the wheels braking under my bunk. The train is pulling into a station. The station is like an island of yellowish light. The light falls on my blanket. It is almost snug, there's almost something reassuring about it—but there isn't anything like snugness or reassurance in my life anymore. One person gets off and walks past the windows. Then the train begins to move again.

Henry's blanket rustles. With his toenail he draws a long line over the mattress, a scratching sound. I think he's raising his head now. His voice sounds clearer, steadier. He's not speaking the words into the pillow so much anymore. As he goes on talking, I can hear him rubbing the pillow with the flat of his hand, as if he were caressing his own soul.

"Anyway, so the three of us were sitting together. Jens had a Coke and an enormous cheeseburger that he was holding pressed together in his pudgy pink hand, the sauce dripping onto the plate. Christine ate some sort of small salad. I only remember how she put the napkin on her lap. How incredibly great it looked! Her movement. The way her hands touched the napkin. And how the napkin lay there. On her thighs. Jens was telling us how he used to spend his summers. He said: 'During summer vacations they always sent me to this health spa on the Baltic to lose weight. Every year. As far back as I can remember. And I really did lose weight, every time. Give or take thirty pounds. But it didn't really work, because I'd gain it all back right away. While I was stuck at this fucking spa, my parents and my sister were always off somewhere on vacation. Like Australia, for instance.' He bit into his cheeseburger. He swallowed and then said: 'When I was born, I already weighed eleven and a half pounds.'

"Christine had pulled a cigarette out of the pack lying on the table. She blew out the match and threw it into the ashtray. Jens took his glass of Coke and raised it to his mouth till the ice cubes clicked against his teeth. After a while I watched a guy and a girl sauntering in, holding hands. They were, like, twenty. The girl followed the guy to the table right next to ours. He sat down. She waited a second and then settled onto the chair. She was really hot. Long blond hair, a short black skirt, a tight white top. She had this small silver tongue ring bobbing between her teeth. The guy had buzzed black hair, a tan, and a hardness about the mouth that was always there, even when the girl giggled and loudly announced that she was so happy, that the day they'd spent together had been real great. I still remember everything so precisely because at some point I looked over at Jens and noticed that he was also watching the two of them. And for the first time I saw that look in his eyes. The one I would later see so many times. That look in which people just have no place. He gazed at the couple for a long while. Then he looked me straight in the eye. He said: 'What being fat boils down to is that everywhere you go, people make fun of you, girls aren't interested in you, and your dad tells you he'll give you a hundred marks for every pound you lose. Believe me, it's fucking great.' He was going to continue, but the waiter came to take away our empty plates. When the waiter left, Jens turned to Christine. 'What do you think, baby face? What's your take on all this?' Christine flicked the ash from her cigarette. 'What am I supposed to think?' she asked. 'That you're nuts?' Christine has this slight French accent. So slight that most people don't even notice.

"'No, I want you to say something for real,' Jens

replied. 'I'm sure baby face can say something for real.' He smiled.

"'Sure thing,' Christine said, raising her voice. 'Baby face can always say something for real. Believe me, the nuts bit *was* for real.' Her eyes were flashing."

Something keeps moving above me in the air. After a while I realize it's Henry's arm dangling down from the bunk above. I look out the window. Outside I can't see a thing.

"You know how people say that nothing lasts," Henry continues, "that everything passes, gets washed away? That nothing follows you eternally on your path? And above all, that you yourself are not eternal? People get angry. You'll hear them say that time should stand still. So that certain things don't get washed away. So that these things are here forever. But what they don't get is that time *has* to go by. That the desire for eternity can only be fulfilled through the passing of time. Time *has* to go by. Things *have* to get washed away. So that you can remember them. So they come alive in your memory. And follow you, maybe forever. The result being that we maybe end up, like, existing for an infinitely long time. You listening?"

"Yeah."

"That challenging flash in her eyes. What's your take—did *that* have to get washed away?"


Oona. My memories of Oona. How old were we—five, six, seven, eight—before she moved? She had brown shoulder-length hair. A sweet, tender face. Pale. Delicate features. Narrow lips. There was something vulnerable about her. Her mother would always doll her up. When I think back, I see little blue ribbons in her hair. I kept going over to her place so we could play with my Masters of the Universe action figures—those plastic monsters you could get at all the department stores. But Oona's parents wouldn't let her play with stuff like that. Her father was home all day because he had some sort of disease that no one was allowed to talk about, and he'd be sitting on the couch in the living room. And I'd always smuggle the action figures under my sweater and take them upstairs to Oona's room. Today, a postcard she sent me is taped to the tiles of my kitchen in Berlin. It shows a vacation house in Sweden. You can't see what's written on the back, but I know it by heart: "Dear

Paul, Sorry it took me so long to answer. Have been rushing about like crazy." I happened to be in her town once. I called her, dropped in to see her. Later I kept leaving messages on her cell phone. She never answered.

Henry says: "We sat in the café a while longer. The waiter brought three cocktails and then left. Christine lit another cigarette. She carefully poked it around in the ashtray, playing with the ashes already in there. Jens had sunk deep into his chair and was looking over at the nutty couple again. I looked at them too. They both had food in front of them—can't remember what. Anyway, the girl asks the guy if she can have the olive on his plate. Jens looked down at a spot in the middle of the table. My eyes focused on his meaty neck, which was almost as wide as his face. He said: 'All the girls go out with real jerks. I know it's a cliché, but it's true. Girls act like the only thing that's important to them is feelings, sensitivity, vulnerability, the soul, and all that stuff, but it's just not true. They get a thousand times more fired up about other things.

Coolness, good looks, rock music. Just like guys. The only difference is that girls always act like it isn't so. That's what's so bad about it. And no way are girls poor, needy, or whatever. At least, not the ones I know. They're calculating and not worth shit.' Jens sucked at his straw, closed his eyes for a moment, and then sucked at it again. I watched the waiter cross the café to the counter and call in an order. 'No way are these girls with these assholes because of some maternal, nurturing instinct,' Jens went on. 'If they really wanted to nurture somebody who needs nurturing, they'd be throwing themselves at me!'

" 'So you're saying that since they're not throwing themselves at you to nurture you, you don't have a girlfriend?' Christine asked, scornfully raising her eyebrows.

" 'Forget it,' Jens said. 'No girl's about to fall in love with someone like me.'

" 'You can bet on it if you keep spouting shit like that,' she said. She took a last drag from her cigarette. Then she stubbed it out in the ashtray. Jens's eyes seemed to fill with sadness for a moment. But then he smiled again. 'Like I care,' he said. 'Who said I even want a girlfriend? Give me a couple of brownies à la mode any day. There were some on the menu, Henry, weren't there?' And he looked around for the waiter."

I have no idea why I started studying ethnology. I guess because it sounded more interesting than other subjects. I'd listen to the lectures, the professor talking about cultural shift in Oceania, and I'd think: that has, like, *nothing* to do with me. Now, while I'm lying here in this train, it seems even further away. And I wish it weren't so far away. Now I wish I could be sitting in a lecture hall again, watching the professor in his linen shirt placing a transparency on the overhead projector. And just take notes.

Henry is silent for a few moments. "You mind if I smoke in here?" he finally asks.

"Go ahead."

I hear him climbing down the ladder from his bunk.

It takes a while for my eyes to make him out. He's only wearing shorts. A few fainter lights wipe past the window. He fishes a pack of cigarettes out of his backpack.

"You want one too?" he asks.

"Sure."

I push back the blanket with my legs and swing myself out of the bunk. He hands me a cigarette and I take it. Then he goes over to the window and opens it, pushing it down by the top of its frame. Cold air comes streaming in. Henry lights my cigarette with a match. A red dot glows in the dark compartment. He lights his cigarette too. Throws the match out into the darkness. I go stand next to him. We stick our heads a few inches out the window.

"You know," he says loudly, "Jens was in love with Christine. I don't think he'd ever loved anyone like that before. He did everything for her. He'd come pick her up from wherever she was and take her wherever she wanted. Can you imagine— when she had a date with some guy, she'd shower and put on makeup and all that at Jens's place. He'd watch her. And then he'd even drive her to her date. I have a feeling she even used to get laid at his place. When he wasn't there, I mean." We pull our heads back into the compartment. My

T-shirt feels ice-cold against my skin. Henry's face is right in front of me. Yet I can't see his eyes. A fanatic, a crazy guy, I suddenly think.

"The twist is that he never told her he was madly in love with her," he says. "Or that he loved her at all."

"Any idea why?" I ask. "I mean, she must have guessed."

Henry takes a drag from his cigarette. "What I figure is, they both, like, totally needed each other. And they both constantly kept lying to each other all the way." He throws his cigarette out into the night. Then he squeezes past me to the shelf, opens one of the two bottles of water, and drinks. The moment he lowers the bottle from his mouth he says: "As for Jens, I reckon nothing frightened him more than rejection." He takes another sip and puts the bottle back on the shelf. "If he'd ever tried to kiss her or something, and she rejected him," Henry continues, "I'm sure he'd have killed himself." He hesitates for a moment before going on. "He tried that twice, you know, overdosing on sleeping pills. And both times he called her first and left a good-bye message on her answering machine."

I too throw my cigarette out the window and push it shut. For a while I just stand there, freezing and lost in thought. Henry is silent too. Finally I ask: "So what did she do?"

"She took a cab and went rushing over—she had the keys to his place. And there he lay. On the floor. His mouth covered in white foam. She called the emergency service and sat by his side in the ambulance as they raced to the hospital. He and baby face."

I feel as if darkness is reaching out and touching my bones. Henry says: "And after the second time, she blew up at him and told him that this was the last time she was coming to save him. But they, like, never talked about their relationship. Her story was that he had bouts of depression. And that was that—things went on just the way they did before. The tragic thing was that I got in the mix."

"If Jens had tried to kiss her," I ask, "do you think she'd have reciprocated?"

"No," Henry replies. "She always told me there was no way she'd ever get involved with Jens. She didn't find him the least bit attractive. The whole thing was just friendship. Nothing more."

He opens the door to the washroom, reaches

inside, and turns on the light. He quickly goes inside and closes the door. The bird is a raven. A pale yellow light shines into the compartment from under the door.

Later, when we're back in our bunks, I ask: "What did Christine do?"

"What?"

"I mean, for a living."

"Quite a lot, actually," Henry replies. "She studied medicine in Brussels. And later on she worked as a French translator for a magazine in Munich."

"And what did you do?"

"I had diarrhea."

"What, all the time? Nothing else?"

"Okay, I was still at school. In twelfth grade. But that was sort of on the side. Mainly I had diarrhea. I felt sick and I had diarrhea. I don't know if it had anything to do with it, but I was also real bad at school. I mean *real* bad. I was always relieved when I managed to pass the exams. I was living with my mother in Munich, in Milbertshofen. My parents got a divorce about three years ago. My mother works at a bookstore, an esoteric bookstore on

Münchener Freiheit. I almost never left my room. When I was there I didn't have to take a shit all the time. I sat at my desk or on my bed and kept jerking off. Or whenever I had a nosebleed, I'd walk around the room staring at the floor, trying to get the blood dripping out of my nose to fall so that some word or image would appear on the floorboards. I always had nosebleeds. And whenever I went somewhere—anywhere at all—I had to take a shit. You know how fucked up that is?"

"Did you see a doctor?" I ask.

"I had hundreds of doctors examine me. Either my mom sent me or I went on my own. Regular doctors, so-called experts, psychologists, holistic practitioners, you name it. None of them could find a thing wrong."

His blanket rustles. "And it was at those school dances, like I told you, that it hit me worst of all. And at clubs. The hatred with which people look at you just because you don't dance, or because you don't dance that well. Or because you're wearing the wrong clothes, or not drinking what they're drinking. Because you don't fit in. Maybe just because you're one more person and they can't handle any more people. Because they're already stepping on each other's toes, already invading each other's spaces, because they keep snatching things away from one another, because they actually want to chase each other off. Somehow everyone has to beat out the other. And there I'd be, sweat pouring from my armpits and running down my sides, my hands clammy, sweat on my forehead, and with such cramps in my stomach that I'd have to run and take a shit right away. Sometimes when I'd be in a public place, or in a bookstore or something, there'd suddenly be such a nasty smell in my nose. Whenever the smell was there, I had the feeling that everything I had shat out, all the blood I had lost with my nosebleeds, had collected somewhere and was about to come crashing over me in a giant wave, and over all the people in the bookstore. I imagined the people being knocked down and washed away, the shelves collapsing under the pressure of the wave. And how everyone would be lying there. In my shit. Sunk in it. I'd be sunk in it too. And just lying there, totally finished."

Silence descends. Henry clears his throat.

"Oh well," he says, "at any rate, I spent most of my time in my room. I felt totally alone. I didn't have a friend or anything. Till I met Jens. When I was with him I felt okay. Maybe because you could see right away that he was lonely too. I guess that was the invisible link that held us together. It made us fellow sufferers in some way. We clung so tightly to each other that we dragged each other right down. But I think I also liked to hang out with him because I never had to put on any kind of act, or pretend I had something more to offer than I did. We got together a couple of times a week. Sometimes just the two of us, without Christine. We'd go to some bar in Schwabing and talk. He'd always come pick me up, and we'd head there in his car. He's got a Citroën Xara, metallic wine red. I tell you, if I saw a car like that now I'd scream."

I hear Henry rubbing one foot against the other. I roll onto my back and stare straight up. Then I clasp my hands together, press them to my mouth, and blow into them. The air warms my fingers. He continues: "We'd always talk about different things. Of course, mainly about Christine. But not exclusively. Once, I remember, we walked down the Leopoldstrasse. It was around eight—a nice, bright summer evening. If someone high up had looked down through an invisible window into the street at all the people there, he'd have thought they were all really happy. Car horns honking, girls' voices hanging in the air. Jens was walking a few paces behind me. I kept turning to look. His walking was more like some sort of stamping. It was as if with every step he wanted to drive his feet into the asphalt. His left arm swung loose by his body. In his right hand he was holding an oily meat loaf sandwich. A napkin was sticking to it. I was waiting for him to eat the thin white paper along with the meat loaf. But he was careful. When nothing but the napkin was left, he crumpled it up and threw it on the sidewalk. His mouth was smeared with mustard. A girl of about twenty was sitting on a step in front of a café. She was wearing a miniskirt, and her knees were pressed tightly together. She had short blond hair and beautiful high cheekbones. She was chewing gum, which brought her cheekbones wonderfully into play. I'd have loved to walk up to her and say: 'Hi. I'm Henry. I exist.' You know that feeling? This incomprehensible urge to walk up to a girl just to let her know that there's someone like you, that you exist? Because the way you see it, your whole world would be better if such a girl knew you existed.

"'Hey, wait a minute, Henry!' Jens had called

out at just that moment. I turned around and went back to him. He was standing in front of the window of a boutique. There was a TV on inside, among the clothes and beautifully dressed mannequins. On the TV, models in the latest Paris fashions were walking in an endless procession along a catwalk. They swayed their hips and turned out their knees as if they were bowlegged. Their legs were terribly thin. Their arms and shoulders too. They were wearing black lipstick. Jens pointed at the screen. 'I just can't stand these images anymore,' he said. 'These girls. These beautiful girls everywhere. On TV, on MTV, in magazines, on billboards. I can't stand it anymore. Those bodies that are so perfect and well formed that you go crazy. And then those girls look at you with such eyes from a screen or a billboard! There's always such an inviting spark in their eyes, such a luring promise: let's dance and burn and fuck till there's nothing left to burn and fuck, till we crumble in black ashes and are scattered in the wind. And all around them there's always this gross, artificial glitter. Though in real life there's nothing, no glitter at all.'

"On the screen, a male model dressed entirely

in black was walking along the catwalk. Enormous black wings were attached to his arms. He stretched them out. Jens went on: 'As if there were some glitter factory somewhere that sends out this glitter shit to the four corners of the earth. A small group of people are working in this glitter factory practically around the clock. For them that's the greatest thing. And other people want to get in at any cost. They'd do anything to get in. Lie in wait by the gates hoping they'll be admitted, ecstatically breathing in the factory fumes. In the meantime, the work in the factory is going on full throttle. Certain issues are invested with an incredible amount of glitter. One issue in particular: sex. Do you know how much I want to fuck? I can barely stand it. I always feel my balls are about to explode—the shock wave strong enough to blast off my legs. And this glitter shit pushes the whole sex thing, complicated as it is, even further out of reach. Everyone acts like they're always having the best sex of their lives. I have no idea if that's true. Anyway, it's a real downer. And everybody always seems to be open to anything when it comes to sex, though at the same time they somehow aren't. They're afraid. And I bet you this being open to everything all the time is real exhausting and that they'd much rather pull back. And they all want to burn and fuck, fuck and burn. Me too. Me too!' Jens stopped talking. He looked at his big, broad reflection in the display window. If you peered through his reflection you could look directly at the screen. The models were still walking."


"You asleep?" Henry asks. I don't answer. I don't feel like answering. I want to think about what he's told me. And I want to think about myself. I shoot the arrows of my thoughts toward Berlin. I've been living there for a year and a half now, and for the most part I've wandered the streets alone. Without having anything to do. I watched people. I know how they open their umbrellas or walk arm in arm, how they march past with absent looks, how their eyes carefully peer at everything, how they buy tickets or run to catch the metro, how they jostle each other or slap each other on the back. How they stop, disoriented, and look around, how they would sit facing me in the metro with furrowed foreheads. All this seemed so familiar, and still these people were so totally alien. I'd just start trailing some people for no reason. Mostly women, of course. And mostly I'd follow them to their front doors. Hours would go by this way. And then I'd realize I hadn't eaten anything all day. I'd forget to eat. Sometimes I'd forget to eat for days in a row. Something stopped me from thinking about food. And I'd feel so weak and empty and sick. There were times when I had to sit down on some stairs or a park bench. I'd feel like I couldn't go on struggling in the whirl of life one second longer. I wanted to grab people by the wrist and turn them around, shout at them, and hit them as hard as I could. But I didn't. I just went on watching them stream past. Sometimes I'd shout something crazy at them. And then I'd finally whisper to myself: "Things go on, they will go on." That's how I spent my days. That's my story. And there's another story. The story I can see in the mirror. In the brown spot in my right eye. Is that you, Mandy?

I take loud, regular breaths because I want Henry to think I'm asleep. Then there's silence. As much silence as there can be in a rattling train. But suddenly he continues with his story. He obviously doesn't care if I'm awake or not. So I keep my eyes open and listen to him.

"Then Jens and I went to Eggers, a café in Hohen-zollernstrasse. The whole way there we walked next to each other without saying a word. Jens kept his eyes fixed on the sidewalk. Eggers has tables outside too, but we wanted to sit inside. We went to a table in one of the corners near a little window. We ordered two Cokes. Jens stared into the window, gazing at the reflections of the people coming into the café. 'I'm too ugly,' he said. He reached for his glass, swirled the Coke in it, and took a sip. Then he leaned back in his chair and looked straight at me. 'That's the way it is,' he said. 'Go on, take a good look at me. I am too ugly to drink a Coke. This Coke should be so freaked by me it should jump right out of the glass. Too ugly to go any-where and meet people.'

"'I don't think you're ugly,' I said. When I said it I meant it. 'And do you know why?' I continued. 'Because you haven't locked your soul in a steel box inside your stomach. Lots of people lock their souls in steel boxes, and keep them locked forever.

You can see it in their eyes. A person's soul shines in his eyes. And all you see in the eyes of people who've locked up their souls is the cold steel of that box. They're the ugly ones. If you ask me, it's an age-old delusion that there's any such thing as a definition of beauty and ugliness. Who has the right to judge who's beautiful and who's ugly? It's true that people have a general idea of what beauty is. And our noses constantly get rubbed in it. Whoever falls through the cracks, whoever is different, is passed over: he's ugly. It's all a big, phony scam that decides between happiness and unhappiness.'

" 'You know what I heard once?' Jens cut in. 'I heard that people who have some kind of handicap, mental or physical, who're stuck in a wheelchair or have a clubfoot, a limp, who have only one arm or can't use their hands, who're blind—I heard that all these people were once space warriors, heroes from other galaxies, creatures of light who were incredibly beautiful and strong and who explored the universe, but who can no longer remember any of it. And the handicaps they have now are the result of their long and difficult journey to earth, the planet that's always been a destination for every space warrior, the place space warriors always get to in the end. Once they're reborn on earth as humans, they're saved. So what I thought was that maybe that goes for fat people too. That fat people were space warriors too. Sounds great, doesn't it? The only reason my face has ended up all bloated is because of that long journey. When it comes down to it, I'm actually a powerful and beautiful creature of light.'

" 'What bullshit!' I replied. "Everyone has some handicap or other. So you're saying that they were all space warriors before they got here? I can't believe the bullshit people talk themselves into, just to feel better. Anyway, the earth isn't much of a destination, is it? I mean, really. Things must be pretty bad in the universe if it's some kind of salvation to end up human.'

" 'You know, if the earth really is a destination,' Jens said, 'and I think how restless I am and how I'm always zipping here and there like crazy, then the expression "Life is a journey, not a destination" rings true.'

"Well, anyway, later on Christine joined us and slumped down exhausted at the table, like she was about to fall asleep. But she didn't get the chance. Jens started quizzing her, the way he often did, about her sex life. If she'd ever tried this or that—questions she could almost always answer with a yes, which she then followed up with a story. She'd tell us how cool it was to use this or that sex toy, alone or with a partner, while she'd always brush a lock of hair out of her eyes or feel the side of her face with her palm, as if to feel her beauty and be reassured. Her words became enticing music. She spoke softly, and as if it was really important to her to somehow bewitch us with her stories. You could see her savoring the way we drooled at some particularly juicy bit in her story. Later that evening the conversation touched on the question of which was greater, sex or food. Christine went for sex, Jens for food. He said: 'The Big Mac is food—and let me tell you, you'd need a hell of a lot of sex toys to put a Big Mac in the shade!'

"And so the days and weeks passed. The three of us would meet in cafés and restaurants, we'd talk, go to the movies, the theater, we'd go on late-night drives in Jens's Citroën Xara while we'd be listening to totally loud music. Or we'd all drive over to my grandma's, where Jens would oversee us cooking some gigantic meal dripping with fat. As we cooked, the music would be blaring too. When I was alone back then, I'd feel totally fucked up. And when I was with the two of them, I reckoned I ought to be happy. But I couldn't feel it. I guess you only feel that kind of thing later. Now I know that I *was* happy back then. I have no idea how the others felt. Sometimes I think I should have seen what was coming. Always when Christine did something on her own—without Jens, and without letting him know—he'd get distant and pissed off. At me too. Even though it had nothing to do with me. It was clear that in his mind we only functioned as a trio. He wouldn't call us or answer his phone. And when we'd hang out again after a while, he'd just sit there without saying a word. He'd sit there with that look on his face, the one I've already told you about. And the crazy thing was that when you'd ask him if he was in love with Christine, he'd go: 'No way. She's the last woman I'd ever fall in love with!' I didn't believe him. I should have seen it all coming."


My newspapers and magazines are *Spiegel, Tagesspiegel, Vogue* (because of the girls). Books from Amazon. You'd be surprised what ends up in our mailbox in Berlin. Sofia always shakes her head. "How can anyone read so much?"

She's twenty-three, and after a shower always comes into the kitchen wrapped in a towel. She's Italian. And she only takes a shower in the afternoon. Nightlife. Soon enough she'll get to cancel all my subscriptions.

Henry says: "There's something else I want to tell you about Christine. There were two things about her that stood out. The first was that she was flawlessly beautiful, from her head down to her toes. The second was that when you met her for the first time, she came across as strangely absent, as if she were looking at the world through a veil. Which was maybe true, as she was really nearsighted. She couldn't even see the Olympic Tower when we were standing right in front of it. I'm serious. But she was too vain to wear glasses. She came across like she wasn't really interested or whatever. Sort of unapproachable. And like with everything you can't approach, it suddenly turns into a challenge: to make Christine laugh, cry, shout, to get her out of that shell of hers. She was drawn to Arab things.

She loved Arab music. I guess she'd have had no trouble walking around in a veil. It would have suited her. Her father was a diplomat. She had traveled all over. She spoke the language of every country she'd lived in—and she'd lived in Brussels the longest. It would totally get on my nerves when she'd be talking French fast on the phone in a high, shrill voice and I didn't get a single word. She'd spend hours putting on makeup. She used foundations, powder brushes, eye shadow, mascara, all kinds of cover sticks, highlighters, and lipsticks. And when she'd come out of the bathroom an hour later, you couldn't even tell she was made up—but she looked great. And her hair shone. She wore a perfume that had something gingery and lily of the valley about it. She always ordered it from Paris, from the same boutique President Mitterand shopped at.

"Another aspect of her personality was her messiness. Wherever she went, there'd be chaos in her wake. Like an animal leaving a trail. Socks, clothes, dirty coffee cups, plates, a leftover spoon, open newspapers, dirty sneakers, a piece of paper covered in her nervous scribble buried under a pile of stuff. I once saw her bring back a suitcase from a trip to a beach resort and never open it. There was still sand on it. She'd never do laundry. The expensive stuff she took to the dry cleaner's, and the rest she'd just throw out and go buy new stuff."

"So, did *you* at least get to tell her that you love her?" I suddenly ask. He doesn't say anything for quite a while. There's a sound of screeching wheels.

"Yes," I finally hear from above. "I did tell her. One evening. In November. It was pouring. When I opened the door, she was standing there dripping wet. She said she'd come to see me and my mother—a sort of surprise visit. But my mother wasn't home. Thank God. Christine came in, threw her sheepskin jacket on the floor, went running to the bathroom, dried her face on a towel, leaned forward, dried her hair as best she could, and then flung it back. I watched her from the hall, fascinated. Then I picked up her jacket and hung it on the coatrack. We went to my room. I had one of those old record players from my dad, on which you could play singles. They were all totally scratched, but sounded great. This warm snugness settles on you whenever you listen to them. And they also kind of reminded me of my dad. We sat on the floor, facing each other. We listened to the old songs. For some of them, the ones I was really into, I showed her the lyrics. I sat down behind her and leaned over her shoulder, pointing at the lines as they were being sung. Like for "The Joker" by the Steve Miller Band. At some point we ordered pizza. It came in, like, twenty-five minutes. Napkins too. As we ate, again sitting face-to-face and listening to the music, I wrote something on my napkin. I wrote: '1. I can't stop looking at you. 2. I love you.'

"I passed the napkin over to her. She read it. The rain was beating against the window. There was a click, and the record came to an end."

"So, how did she react?" I ask, raising my head in his direction.

"At first she didn't say anything," Henry replies in a low voice. "Then she said: 'You're too young.'"

"And then what?"

"She told me that time was 'on my side.' That there was something special about me. And that when I was older she was sure a lot of women would go for me. And fall in love with me. But I can't say I was jumping with joy. She walked over to the window and looked out into the rain. After a few moments she turned and looked at me again.

And then, to lighten the silence that had sprung up between us, she began to talk in general about 'time as such.'"

"Time as such?" I ask, and then with a touch of irony add: "Isn't that your favorite topic?"

"Yes," Henry says with a deep sigh. "It is my favorite topic. I was so upset that it was a miracle I even managed to follow her line of thought. She said: 'It's, like, time shows no consideration for an individual's destiny—it devours everything equally. But there's more to it than that. Time, like, *does* think about you for a long, long while before you are in a position to think about time. And time prepares things for you. Think about how much time had to get ready so that you could even exist. And all the while time was also preparing all the places you would be in during your life.'

"'Do you mean that to some extent all the places I'll ever be in sort of exist the way they do just for me?' I asked her in surprise.

"'Of course,' Christine replied. 'To some extent.'

"'That means time must be sort of interested in the fact that I exist,' I said.

"'Exactly,' she said. 'Time is like a servant who can tell far in advance that her master is getting tired, and so she goes off to get his bed ready for him. The only difference between the servant and time is that the servant serves her master constantly and exclusively, while time seems to serve only itself, refusing to follow anyone's instructions. It's kind of like time makes the bed for somebody so that time itself can lie down in it by way of that person. Though I have no idea what it is that time might be preparing by the fact that you and I exist.'

"My mother turned up at some point, and we all went into the living room to talk. My mother was going on about some healing stone that Christine should put under her bed. It would do her good. An onyx. It would establish a superior harmony between her core and her outer shell, and all that. And a superior zest for life. Great. After an hour and a half Christine left. I spent the rest of the evening lying on my bed staring out into the rain. The onyx under my pillow didn't make *me* feel any better. Not to mention," Henry adds, "that Christine went straight over to Jens and told him how I'd come on to her. And then he told me that at least it was clear now why I had always been bugging him about whether he was in love with Christine or not. And he began giving me nutty, older-brother tips on how to win her over. It's all weird, if you think about it."

The pictures are all bogus. The pictures that make me crazy, that turn me on, that I jerk off to. I saw a documentary on TV about how they doctor those pictures. A computer elongates the women's legs, their butts become rounder, their tits larger, their eyes are made a swimming-pool blue. *Look at me! I want to get into your blood! I want to alter your genes! To control them! Be like me! Seek me in reality!* The pictures are everywhere. But the horniness they beget pours into nothingness.

"I'm feeling cramped in here," Henry says suddenly. "Want to go out into the corridor for a while?"

"Sure, let's go."

I think it's a great idea. Besides, I need a quick change of air. I'd rather be alone, but you can't have everything. Henry climbs down the ladder from his bunk. A dim light is burning in the corridor. You can't see anything of the landscape outside. You can only see yourself. But when I look at myself in the reflection, I look into a deeper darkness than the one outside. Henry and I go and stand in front of the window. It's weird to be able to see his face clearly again. He gazes with sad eyes at something unreal beyond his reflection. He crosses his arms over his thin, bare chest. Suddenly one of the nearby compartment doors opens, and two giggling girls come stumbling out into the corridor. One of them sways, drops her half-empty glass, and goes crashing to the floor. She rolls onto her back, laughing loudly. The other girl looks at us apologetically. "She's had too much to drink," she says, and tries to pull her friend onto her feet again. They disappear back into their compartment. Only her glass remains outside on the floor. They were pretty, those two. I had noticed them just after I got on the train. Henry looks at me. There's a faint smile about his lips.

"You can't imagine how into them I am," he says.

"What, those two?"

"Yeah, those two as well," he replies. "All girls. I can hardly stand it. It eats up my days and nights. I'm crazy about girls. They're the greatest thing in the world. There's this superior, celestial quality about everything they do. It's like the ground itself had taught them how to walk on it, like the wind had taught them how to run their fingers through their hair, and like the stars had shown them what distance means. It's as if fire had taught them how to burn. And not only to burn—fire has also taught them how to make sparks fly."

"And alcohol has taught them how to hit the floor," I say.

"Shut the fuck up," he says, and laughs. "They're really like that, and I love them. But you know what's crazy about it?"

"What?"

"That at the same time I want to kill them, in a, like, really brutal way. All of them." He stares at me for a second and then lowers his eyes.

"How come?" I ask.

"Because they're so fucking arrogant. They think the world revolves around them. That everything's bright and beautiful just because they're sitting there brushing a lock of hair out of their eyes. And they always make you feel like you have to do something God knows how special even to be allowed into their presence. But there's no way you can manage it. I for one can't."

"You talk just like that fat guy, Jens," I say. "Every girl's totally different. The only thing they have in common is that they're people like everyone else. That's what's important. I think they really want to be seen as people, not like some celestial being. Can you imagine the pressure that puts on them? Think how hard it must be to live up to being celestial all the time when you were born here on earth. Imagine what it must be like if people expect that every time you take a step it looks as if the ground itself had taught you how to walk. If it was me, I'd never move my legs again. You're saying we have to do something God knows how special just to be allowed in their presence? The way I see it, it's the exact opposite. *They're* the ones who achieve something really special—and it's us who demand that they do."

Henry hangs his head between his shoulders. He is silent. He is silent for a long time. The train takes a curve.

"So they are celestial beings after all," he finally says with a smile.

"Sure," I reply, and take a deep breath. "They are celestial beings after all." We grin at each other.

"You know what I think?" he says after a while.

"What?"

"I think," he says, "that we all need protection from the pigs with wings floating past our window."

"What pigs?"

"Pigs that scare us as they fly past. They're huge. Black. Like, their hide's totally burnt and their wings are covered in white feathers. And they look at you with nasty, burning, red eyes."

"What do those pigs do?"

"No idea," Henry says. "Maybe they're a sign of something. Maybe they're some kind of messengers that come to tell you that your soul is damaged. Or that you're about to go insane. The only thing to do is to draw curtains over the window so you can't see them anymore. And so they can't see you. So that you're protected."

"But maybe there's a reason for us to see them," I say. "Because they're here to warn us about something. Maybe they don't mean us any harm. They just look at us fiercely. Because we don't really have any conviction in ourselves. It could be that these pigs come from inside us. And that that's the reason we're so scared of them. But you know, there isn't just one window we can look through — there are thousands of them. Maybe these pigs belong behind this one window along with all the other terrible beasts living inside us. A window through which they can't escape, and draw attention to themselves, frightening us to death. But they have to be visible. You have to know that they're there, that they're part of you."

"No way," Henry says with conviction. "I don't want them to be there. And no way are they part of me. I don't want to see them, either. I guess you can't even picture what a terrible sight they are. I want to protect myself from them." He throws his hands up in the air. Then he lets them drop. He frowns at the glass lying on the ground. He seems to want to say something more. But he only sucks his lower lip between his teeth.

"Let's go back inside," he says after a long pause.


Later, when we're back in our bunks, I say: "There's something I wanted to ask you. Was there another reason why Jens was so fat? Other than eating so much?"

"No," he replies. "He just ate too much. He ate and ate. He was so fat that sometimes I got embarrassed walking with him in the street. He always had food in his hand: a candy bar, a bagel, a meat loaf sandwich, a bag of honey-coated almonds. And you could tell what the people in the street were thinking: like he needs it, the fat pig! Whenever he came to pick me up from school and stood outside in the school yard, I was embarrassed. Because everyone saw I had a fat friend. Who didn't look good. Not the best thing for one's rep. I was embarrassed and felt really sorry for him because I was embarrassed. It was mean of me. On the one hand, I needed him really badly. Because he was the only one who was always there for me, who didn't jerk me around, with whom I felt safe. But on the other hand, I'd have preferred a cool friend I could be proud of. Know what I mean?"

"Sure."

Henry goes on, his voice softer: "Whenever he was upset as a little boy, his grandma would comfort him. She'd always cook him something. Something sweet. He loved his grandma. I guess if he had someone who really loved him now—a girl, I mean—then maybe he'd stop stuffing himself with food. I think he hates his body."

Henry clears his throat. He suddenly changes the subject.

"We're completely alone," he says. There is sadness in his voice.

"You mean in here?" I ask. "In this compartment? We're not alone. There's two of us."

"No, I mean in general. In the world. Everyone's alone. Even if you're with someone else in a compartment, you're still alone."

"What the hell are you talking about?" I say. "That's got nothing to do with anything."

"It does," Henry replies. "It has something to do with me."

"Jesus!" I wish *I* were alone, I think—alone.

"What?" Henry asks.

"Nothing. I'm just tired. Tell me more."

"Really?"

"Sure."

"You know, when I was a little boy and felt lonely, I'd tell myself that I wasn't really alone. And you know why? Because I'd imagine that there was something, like, following the plot of my life."

"You mean God?"

"No, not God. But not a person, either. Some being. Many beings. And I'd imagine that they were all really excited about me and that they were always on pins and needles about what would happen next. I imagined that they all loved me, the way you love a character in a book. That I'm their hero. That they cheer me on through difficult situations. And can empathize with me. I had no idea how that might work, or how these beings could follow my life all the time. But I didn't give it all that much thought. I was just convinced that they were somehow with me. And that was comforting."

"Wow, that's great."

"No, it isn't. It's just stupid. Nobody follows the story of our lives. Because it doesn't matter what we do—nobody applauds when we've done something, something we think is great, at least when it happens. And you know, even if someone did applaud, if everyone applauded, if they really did, jumping to their feet and going crazy, you'd still feel alone, maybe even more so."

"How about if you applaud yourself?" I say. "After all, you're the only person who follows yourself throughout your life. No one else will follow you wherever you go. And no one else knows you as well as you do, knows your fears, your diarrhea, knows what's hard for you."

"Why do souls have to be trapped in different bodies?" Henry says. "Why can't they be together? Flowing into a single stream, everything flowing together. No more loneliness."

"There must be a reason for it being the way it is. Maybe a single eternal stream would be too boring. It's great that life is so complex. That nothing's like anything else, that every creature is unique. That you are unique."

"Yeah, right."

"Well, it might sound crazy, but the way I see it life has managed things so that in the long run it all does merge together." I hesitate for a moment, and then add: "And when the time comes for me to merge with something, then I sure want to merge with the hottest girls. And they won't be able to do anything about it."

"You're a fucking idiot," Henry says, laughing. "How about trying to merge with them now, not sometime in the future?"

.   .   .

A short stop at a station. Light falls into the compartment, until the train moves on. Into the night.

Henry says: "We were planning to spend a weekend at Jens's parents' place. They've got a big house near Regensburg. The three of us were in the car listening to a tape of the Who. Jens was driving, Christine was next to him, their shoulders moving to the music, and they would yell out at some of the songs. I sat in the back, also moving to the music and yelling. Rock music is the greatest, I thought. These totally old songs. We'd listen to them all the time. I think the three of us would have liked to be young in some other generation.

"Traffic on the autobahn was bad—it was December, and it was iced over in some places. None of us imagined what was going to happen that night. When we got to the house we were greeted by this incredible meal that Jens's grandma had cooked. Then we went to the Christmas fair with his parents. I bought Christine a gingerbread heart. I kept walking behind her so I could watch her walk. It started to snow. The snowflakes hung beautifully in her hair. It was like she was related to the snowflakes, like she was made of many, many tiny snow crystals. Whenever we stopped at a booth, I would rest my chin on her shoulder. It was a beautiful, cold afternoon. We were all in a great mood. Later that evening we went up to Jens's room. The TV was on. We watched a show in which people called in to discuss their problems with a bunch of psychologists. Maybe we should've called in too.

"Jens's bed had been made up for Christine, and us guys were to sleep next to it on two mattresses on the floor. But I didn't sleep. I just couldn't bear Christine being so near. I kept thinking how she was lying there practically naked under the blanket. It was fucking dark in that room. I lay on my back, my eyes wide open, and stared up at the ceiling. I couldn't see a thing. I was all keyed up. I was sweating. I thought the blood would spurt from my head. A howl broke loose in me, which stayed trapped inside. The howl of some disgusting creature cowering inside my body: me. And I was afraid. Fucking terrified. Of everything in the world. Of life. Suddenly I felt this fear very clearly.

Fear, the queen of all feelings. I wanted to go over
to Christine. I thought of my life. Of my fucking
future. Of how I had no idea what life was all
about. Of how everyone says you have to be good.
Always. Everywhere. In all things. That it's so hard
not to lose yourself in the depths of the blue sky
during the day. And in the depths of the sky's blackness during the night. But I wasn't good. I just
wasn't. I wanted to go over to Christine. I suddenly
didn't care that I didn't know what life was about. I
didn't care that Jens was there in the room too. I
just wanted to go to her. The queen of all feelings
could kiss my ass, could feed me to her crocodiles.
I wouldn't have cared shit. As long as I was with
Christine. I wanted to fuck her. I wanted to fuck
her real bad. I couldn't stand it. I wanted to merge
with the snow crystals. Till they melted. Jens was
snoring loudly next to me. His snoring sounded
like a rasp, starting with a jolt and then breaking off
for a few seconds. At some point he let loose a, like,
really funny, drawn-out snore. Muffled giggling
came from Christine's bed. It's now or never, I
thought. I threw back my blanket. Got up. I felt
sick. I tapped my way through the dark room,
stretching out my hands. As if I was a bat covered in

sensors that can feel obstacles before bumping into them. Behind me, snoring. A relief, as I knew that Jens was asleep and wouldn't catch on to what I was up to. Finally my eyes got used to the darkness. The objects took on gray outlines. Christine's bed, the chair standing in front of it. I sat down on the chair and held my breath. The snoring stopped. I saw the contour of Christine's body on the bed. She was lying curled up on her side, her face toward me. Her face shimmered in the dark. I wanted to touch her forehead, and carefully reached out my hand. When I found it, I brushed my index and middle fingers over it. Again and again. She slid a little closer. I leaned forward and breathed in the air above her skin. I thought that from now on I would only breathe where her skin breathed. Then I leaned back. I suddenly had incredible cramps in my stomach. I fought back the urge to rush to the toilet. I tightened up my stomach. I felt totally gross. Especially in comparison to her. And suddenly I got real mad at her. Because she just lay there, so wonderful. She didn't give a shit about me. She'd said I was too young. Too young for what? To fall in love with her? To fuck her? Was I also too young to rape her? I wanted to grab her, tear her around, get her hot, crazy hole where I wanted it, and then fuck her. I didn't care if she wanted to or not." Henry is silent for a moment. Then he asks: "Have you ever been on a beach at night when everything's dark and you can't see a thing? When you feel the sand beneath your feet but can't see it? And you feel the cool wind blowing off the sea, and hear the waves rolling in and crashing onto the sand? Did you ever have the urge, like me, to shout at the thundering dark sea? God knows why. You know that feeling?"

"I know that feeling," I say quietly.

He continues: "That was precisely the feeling I had that night as I sat on that fucking chair. Everything came out sadness. And I sat there with my hard-on pressing against my sweat-drenched shorts, and I started caressing her forehead again. She slid closer and closer to me. She took hold of my hand and slowly drew it down her nose to her mouth. My fingers brushed her lips and she opened them and I felt her tongue. She let my hand slip downward. Over her breasts, her stomach. Everything felt so soft and smooth. Till we got to where I wanted to go. And where she wanted me to go. Between her legs. It was so wonderfully wet down there. You could tell through her panties. I could also feel her pubic hair. I brushed my hand over it. Only the delicate cloth of her panties lay in between. Like soft skin. Maybe this is crazy, but the way I see it, it's worth being alive just to get to touch something like that. I slid my finger into her panties. Pulled them slightly away from her skin. Then I slid my whole hand beneath her panties. My head was on fire. I was shivering. You can't imagine how warm and seething her pussy was. I wanted to be part of that seething then and there. To dissolve. But still be here. To live. Within her. 'You're pinching me,' she whispered. A cold shudder slithered down my back. She turned away from me, so that she was lying with her back to me. I thought: fuck, how am I going to get into bed with her without letting go of her body? And without pinching her? I somehow managed. I tried to pull her panties down, and she helped me, I could feel her helping me. Through the movements of her ass. Dear God, please, please don't let me get the shits now! I thought. I was so scared I'd get diarrhea that I didn't dare take off my shorts. But my dick jutted out on its own. I clasped her stomach in my arms and pressed her tightly against me. I almost shot when her buttocks pressed against my dick. And rubbed against it. Her buttocks were all wet. Her whole body was wet. And mine too. She opened her legs a little. My dick was still rubbing against her ass. I slipped a little lower, poking around, till she reached behind her, grabbed it, and guided it to the right place. I slowly slid it in. Slid it in as deep as it would go, and then we really started. Right away I squirted a little. I held on to her tight. I had the feeling I was sliding in butter. My head was pounding. Pounding like crazy. Bolts of lightning flashed through my body. I knew I never wanted to stop. Never. It was rough and slippery at the same time. Christine's ass was undulating. And there was somehow a buttery aroma. A smell of pastries. Christmas pastries. I slid my hands under her T-shirt. I grabbed her tits and pressed them together. Her two nipples stuck out stiff between two fingers of each of my hands. She moaned lightly. And I wanted to go on like this for the rest of my life. But I couldn't bear it. Everything was so warm, my dick was sliding up and down in butter, Christine's ass moved faster and faster, my heartbeat pounded in my ears, my knees shivered, my whole body contracted, I couldn't hold back, and just as a loud voice right next to the bed yelled, 'Fucking shit!' I shot my load."

Henry continues his story: "It was Jens's voice. Of course. Who else? I'd forgotten all about him. She obviously had too. It took quite a while for me to realize what had happened. He'd already rushed out of the room. Our bodies separated. My heart was beating painfully fast. My dick and underwear felt sticky. Christine jumped up, stood in front of the bed, and kept saying to herself, 'In his bed, in his bed of all places!' She said: 'We have to go talk to him. You lead the way, I can't see a thing.'

"'What're we going to say?' I asked.

"'We'll think of something,' she replied. 'But we gotta talk to him.'

"I led the way out of the room. I had no idea where we were going or where he could be. Nor did I want to fling open some door and end up in his grandma's or parents' bedroom. Christine, behind me, laid her hand on my shoulder. It was completely dark. We felt our way down the stairs. We found him lying on the living-room floor. Like an enormous sack. I leaned over him and tapped his shoulder.

"'Leave me alone!'

"I told him I was sorry. Christine also told him she was sorry. He didn't answer. We went back upstairs. I got into bed next to her and pressed myself against her as tightly as I could.

"The next day Jens didn't say a word. We drove home without rock music, without talking. Jens didn't call the next couple of weeks, either. He didn't have to leave his apartment, since he has loads of food stashed away, enough to last him a few weeks."

There's a long pause. My thoughts travel down repulsive dream paths. Then his voice brings me back to the compartment. "You awake?" he asks me.

"Yeah."

I look outside. Large snowflakes crash against the window, stick for a while, and then slither downward as they melt. I think of how cold it is outside. It's warm in the compartment. But I still feel cold.

"Can you imagine how disgusting it is to have diarrhea, all the time and everywhere?" I suddenly hear him say. "When you can hardly go anywhere anymore?"

"No, I can't imagine," I say. "Why don't you stop going on and on about your diarrhea!"

"You see, that's the problem," he says. "Nobody wants to hear about my diarrhea, not even the doctors. Whenever I go to a doctor, he just tells me to take Perenterol, before I can even explain that it doesn't help."

We're both quiet again. After a while he clears his throat.

"Paul, what's the meaning of love?" he asks.

"Love is pain," I reply. "Excruciating pain."

"That's it?"

"That's it."

"I don't agree," he says. "I think love is the greatest thing in the world, the most wonderful thing there is. A magical elixir of life. The thing that all our longing is made of. If you think about it, we're always longing for love. And everything we do, we do to get love. And love also means not being scared anymore. Not of yourself. And not of other people, either." He hesitates. "This fucking fear, this fucking fear that swallows you up," Henry suddenly says angrily. "Why can't we just handle things coolly and confidently? It would be so much easier, and we'd actually get somewhere."

"Not if you ask me," I say. "Fear can make you think fast in tough situations, it can help you find a way out. Unless it makes you freeze, like a rabbit in front of a snake. I guess there's that too. And that's bad. But otherwise fear can be a help."

"You think so?"

"Sure. Not to mention that there has to be something like fear, otherwise you wouldn't know what coolness and confidence are. Everything's connected. You always need the opposite, the other side of something, just to know that that something even exists. Without darkness, you wouldn't know what light is. There are actually people who believe that God created the universe so He could see Himself—the way we talk with another person, because we define ourselves through other people. Because we can only realize what *we* are like through the way *they* are. And God can only realize who or what He is through the universe. That's why He created it."

"If that's true, then that means that God is like us."

"Yes."

"Just as helpless."

"Maybe He *is* just as helpless."

We fall silent.

"Is God lonely?" he asks after a while.

Admiralstrasse. Walking down Admiralstrasse. The tall, barren trees. Villas behind front gardens on both sides of the street. Streets don't tell their secrets. I know Admiralstrasse only at night. I wonder if Henry, lying above me in the dark, will also walk down Admiralstrasse. Perhaps during the day. Nor can you see the secrets of passersby on a street.

Henry says: "There are lots of people who can't accept gifts, who don't like getting a gift. Their conscience bothers them, and they feel like they have to reciprocate. They feel they don't deserve to get something without giving something back. I think it's kind of the same with life. Life is something that you were given. And some people can't accept the gift of life, just like they can't accept smaller gifts.

They feel like they don't deserve to be alive. They're totally desperate. They torture themselves. Some even kill themselves. Because reciprocating the gift of your life is a terrible task. It can't actually be done. Even if you could reciprocate—who would you reciprocate to? God? Your parents?"

He gives it some thought. Then he goes on: "But aren't presents a sign of affection too? When you're given the present of living, isn't that also a sign of affection? Doesn't the fact that you're here also somehow mean that you deserve to be alive? That you're valuable enough? But why don't you ever feel valuable? And almost nobody ever thinks you are valuable."

There is silence for a few moments. "You know," he suddenly says joyfully, "it's a fact that most people in the world are unhappy. But I don't want to be unhappy. Not anymore. I've had enough. In this one thing I wouldn't mind belonging to a minority for a change."

I remember: one evening I was riding on the Berlin metro. I was going from Charlottenburg to

Friedrichstrasse. A girl got on at Bahnhof Zoo and sat down near me. She pulled up her legs and put her feet up on the seat opposite. Her head sank against the window. She fell asleep. She had curly black shoulder-length hair. Her face was so serene. Like she was having a beautiful dream. I didn't get off at Friedrichstrasse. I stayed on the train till it reached the final stop. She was still asleep. I touched her shoulder. "Wake up," I said in a low voice. "This is the last stop."

Startled, she opened her eyes. A few seconds passed.

"What were you dreaming about?" I asked her. She didn't answer. She jumped up, grabbed her bag, and ran out. I ran out too.

"What were you dreaming about?" I shouted after her. "What were you dreaming about?"

Henry continues his story: "Four days after our trip, after that night, I got together with Christine in a Greek restaurant. She looked great—really hot. She was wearing a black T-shirt, black jacket, and black pants. She always wore something black. She knew it suited her. She ordered an apple soda and eggplant stuffed with goat cheese. I ordered an orange Coke and a gyro with rice. We sat there silently for a long time. At some point she said that she wished we hadn't done what we did. That it shouldn't have happened. And wouldn't happen again. That it was her fault. I couldn't go on eating, but she chatted on about how she'd been at the movies the day before. The movie hadn't been good, I shouldn't bother going to see it. I sat there unable to say a word, feeling like shit. And she didn't even notice that I wasn't saying anything. When we left the restaurant and said good-bye, she called out, 'Okay, see you!' and hurried off in her high heels. I went home. My mother met me at the door and told me to unload the dishwasher. You could tell she was pissed off that I hadn't done it before going out. I ran up to my room and slammed the door. 'I'll do it later!'"

He lets his hand hang down again. "I just couldn't deal with Christine's attitude. I mean, why would she sleep with me, and after all that just jabber on the way she did?"

"Because she felt lonely, because she was in the mood that night," I reply. "Women are just as much into fucking as we are. They sometimes act like they're not, but they are."

"Great," he says.

The yellow ball. On the squash court, the color of the ball indicates how good you are. Valentin and I play yellow. Quite good. Instead of military service Valentin opted for community service and is working at Berlin's Charité Clinic, in orthopedics. He's a satellite in my life. Always in the same orbit. Same place, same time, same distance. A small, stocky satellite that sometimes says, "I wish I were like you."

You ought to be able to talk with friends. He talks a lot as he drinks his apple soda after the game. He's not like me.

Henry's standing at the open window again. Smoking. With his back to me. I stay in my bunk because I'm too cold. The ash of his cigarette glows. The train is rattling.

"I can't go on with the story," he says. "I can't talk about it anymore."

"So lie down and try and get some sleep."

"Can't do that, either." He's silent for a while. Then he says: "I didn't hear from Jens over the holidays. I guess he was with his parents. I didn't hear from Christine, either. I only knew she'd moved out from my grandma's and into a one-bedroom apartment in Munich. A wall of silence had risen between us. It was like the three of us had never existed. And then today, a few days after New Year's, Jens suddenly knocked at my door. I opened, and he just walked in without a word. He went to my room; I followed him. He sat down on my bed and began to cry. He cried and cried and cried. He just wouldn't stop. A quaking and quivering colossus. He held his pudgy pink hands over his face. He was sweating. Sweat was running down his neck and under his collar. I knew it had something to do with Christine. I just didn't know what. I sat down next to him. 'What happened?' I asked. Jens pulled his shirt out of his pants and wiped his eyes with his shirttail. Blew his nose in it. Then he began to talk. He wasn't really talking—the words just came bursting out. 'She never wants to see me again. She said she never wants to see me again.'

"'Why?'

"'I don't know,' he replied. 'I have no idea.'

"He coughed. For a while we sat on my bed in silence. I laid my hand on his shoulder. He looked at me. I suddenly realized he wasn't seeing me, I wasn't even there. The eyes that were looking at me were no longer his. They were turned inward. His look freaked me out. Something terrible was lurking behind his eyelids. Then he suddenly got up, grabbed my wrist so that it hurt, and said: 'We'll go get her stuff that's still at my place and take it to her. Both of us.' It was an order. We got into his car and he drove over to his place, his hand still gripping my wrist—I had to get out on his side with him. We went into his apartment, the apartment in which the three of us had spent so much time, where the floor was always dusty and there was always a mess. The moment we were inside, Jens pulled a box from under his bed and opened it. I felt my stomach turn. The box was full of things belonging to Christine: a small red toothbrush, panties, a blouse, a used washcloth, a half-empty bottle of perfume, a comb with hairs stuck to it, faxes, postcards . . . I was, well, pretty freaked out. Someone secretly collecting someone else's personal items. And then he tells me to my face: 'This is my *Christine box*.' He holds it to his chest like it's the most precious thing he has. Then he says: 'Call her!' So I did. First I called her editorial office, but one of her colleagues told me she'd left for the day.

"'Call her at her place!' he said. And I did.

"'Hello?' It was her. But her voice sounded different.

"'Hi there, it's me, Henry. I—'

"She cut in: 'Henry, where are you?'

"'I'm at Jens's. He wants to bring you your stuff. I—'

"'What stuff? I don't want anything. If I left anything at his place he can throw it out.' Her voice was quaking. I had never heard her in such a state. She started shouting. 'And I'd get the hell out of there if I were you! I'm black-and-blue all over. He beat me up. He went at me like an animal!'

"Jens was standing in front of me, and while she told me this I kept looking at his face.

"'Get the hell out of there!' she shouted again and hung up.

"'She doesn't want her stuff back,' I said quickly. He didn't reply. Then he said: 'We're going over to her place now.'

"He grabbed me by the wrist again and pushed

me out of the apartment, the box under his arm. We got in his car again and he immediately stepped on the gas. His face got all scrunched up. He was getting more and more freaked. We came to a red light. He drove right through it. A driver jammed on his brakes. Jens started speeding like a lunatic. I was so fucking relieved when he finally pulled up in front of Christine's apartment block. I had no idea what he had in mind. We got out. He said: 'Take this box up to her—I'll wait here.' I did as he ordered. I took the elevator up to the fourth floor and went to her door. I rang. The door remained shut, but I could hear someone breathing on the other side.

"'Christine?' I said. 'It's me, Henry. I'm alone.'

"She opened the door, and quickly locked it behind me. She looked dreadful. It was obvious she'd been beaten up. Her face and arms were heavily bruised. She was crying. Her hair hung tattered down into her face—I'd never seen it like that before. Jens had turned up at her office a few hours back. She'd been alone in there. He'd locked the door and started tearing through the office like a wild animal. He grabbed her hands, shook her, slapped her, threw her against the wall. Grabbed her breasts, tore off all her buttons. She started shouting. She was scared to death. Someone in the office heard her and began pounding on the door.

"'I managed to get the door open from inside,' she said. 'A colleague came in, and Jens ran out.' She shook as she spoke. From head to toe.

"'You'd better be careful,' she burst out. 'He's totally flipped. I have no idea what he's going to do. I yelled after him that I never wanted to see him again. Ever. That I'd call the police if he ever turned up.' Exhausted, she slumped down into a chair. 'I don't know what's gotten into him,' she continued. 'He sent me a fax, asking me why I hadn't called him yesterday, what kind of a friend I was. You know, he once knocked his father out. Just like that. Because things weren't going his way. I never told you that. He's insane, Henry. He's really insane. Stay away from him.' She stood up, handed me back the box, and said, 'Throw it in the garbage downstairs.'

"I went to the door, opened it, and there was Jens. Right in front of me. Christine pushed me out with a shout and slammed the door shut. I heard her lock and bolt the door. I looked at Jens. Everything went silent. As if the moment had frozen solid. There was no trace of humanity in his face, nothing familiar. His face was red, his eyes almost white. I thought he would kill me—he's going to kill me right this minute. I ran past him as fast as I could, down the stairs. I heard him get in the elevator. I ran, tossing the box with Christine's things right there in the stairwell. I heard the humming of the elevator. I ran. When I got to the lobby he was there waiting for me. He dragged me to his car with an iron grip. I had to get in, I had no choice. I was sweating with fear, with terror. I wanted to jump out. But he drove off. He was just staring through the windshield. He stepped on the gas pedal. Streetlights, cars, he didn't care about a thing.

"'I'm going to kill myself,' he said. 'But I'm going to take as many people as I can with me. You too. I'm heading for the autobahn—I'm going to head down the wrong way. Sounds good, right? Or should I do the sidewalk?' He tore the steering wheel around. Drove right up to the sidewalk. 'Take a look at them—look at all those fuckwads!' he said, pointing at the people on the sidewalk. They were mainly young people. 'You're not going to tell me that any of those would be a great loss. Or that you or I would be a great loss. No one is. Come on, we'll drive over to my place. I've got a big carving knife at home. We can play a game. First, I get to ram the knife into some part of your body. And then you can do the same with me. We'll keep taking turns, the way buddies do. And we'll keep playing till one of us dies. We won't stop till the end. I won't let you stop.'

"I could no longer think straight. Suddenly he started bawling as he sat there at the wheel. He reached over to me. 'You're my friend, right?' he said. 'Friendships are important, aren't they? More important than anything else. Friends always stay together.' His voice cracked. 'This fucking car doesn't go over a hundred and ten!' He slammed his fist on the speedometer. I had the crazed hope that the police would turn up and stop us. A car tearing down Leopoldstrasse, swerving into Hohenzollernstrasse with screeching wheels, must be stopped by the police. Usually they're on every fucking corner. Pedestrians were jumping out of the way, shouting. Jens didn't hear a thing, didn't see a thing. Suddenly he slammed on the brakes. He sat there stock-still for a few seconds. Then he said: 'Let's go for a drink.'

"He left the car where it was, turned on the hazard lights. I walked with him into a café, my knees shaking. We sat at a table. He said in his normal voice: 'You're all I have left. My only friend. If you leave me, I'll be lost.' I avoided his eyes and said, 'I've got to go to the men's room.' As I closed the door and stood in the dark hallway that led to the toilets, I felt I had finally escaped. I ran through a side door out into a yard and onto the street. I ran and ran and ran. Along the way I got stomach cramps. But this time I hardly noticed them. I only noticed later that I'd shat my pants. I wasn't even embarrassed. I didn't care. I just had one thought, one urge: to run. But I suddenly stopped. I thought of Christine. I wanted to go to her. Nowhere else. I had to. At all costs. I didn't even know the way to her place. But I wasn't thinking. I just ran and ran. I had to get there as fast as I could. I wanted to talk to her, be near her, protect her. I had no idea if Jens was already on his way there. Or if he was there already, waiting for me. I had never run like that before. I ran through half the town. In my soiled pants. Till I finally got to her street and saw her apartment block. I stopped for a few seconds in her stairwell, gasping for air. I pressed the elevator button, but the elevator didn't come. I ran up the stairs, two by two. I kept yelling out her name. I got to her door and started hammering on it.

"'Christine!' I yelled. 'It's me! Are you there? Christine!' I could tell she was standing behind the door.

"I heard her voice. 'Where is he?'

"'I don't know,' I replied, glad that he wasn't with her. 'I managed to get away from him. Open up.'

"She didn't reply.

"'I love you,' I suddenly said. 'I love you so much. I don't know what to do or where to go. I just know I want to be with you. Forever. I'll never leave you, Christine. Believe me. There's no place for me to go. There is no place for me without you. I want to be with you.'

"I pounded on the door with my fists.

"'You hear me, Christine! Let me in!'

"'He'll be coming over here,' she said.

"'I don't care,' I replied quietly, and then whispered, more to myself than to her, 'I'm with you. I'll stay with you.'

"I caressed the door, and then leaned my back against it and slowly slid down, until I was sitting on the floor. The shit in my pants was squished up against my ass. My ass was burning.

"'Aren't you going to let me in?' I asked again.

"'It's all over, Henry,' she said from the other side of the door. 'It's all over.' But I didn't really hear her. Her voice sounded muffled and somehow very far away.

"'God, Christine,' I stammered, 'God, how I love you.'

"'He's going to come here,' she said. 'Stay away from him! And stay away from me! If he comes here, I'm calling the police. And if he comes to your place, I'd do the same. Henry? Are you there?'

"I jumped up and pounded on the door. 'Open up!' I shouted. 'Open the door!' I began to cry. Tears ran down my face. My eyes went bleary. I could see the door only as something white and shimmering before me. I pounded it with my fists until my bones cracked and I felt a dreadful pain. But I continued pounding.

"'Let me in!' I yelled. 'Let's find a place where we can be together, where we won't be alone. There's got to be such a place. We'll find it. Together. Open the fucking door!'

"'Didn't you hear what she told you?' I now

heard a man's voice from behind her door. I didn't recognize the voice. 'You'd do better to go home. There's nothing you can do here. Christine's okay now. It's all over, you hear? It's over.'

When the voice went quiet, I said nothing. I just stood there. Then I turned around and slowly went down one step, then another, and finally ran all the way down. What would you have done?"

I'm a joker, I'm a smoker, I'm a midnight toker, I play my music in the sun, I thought. Old songs, Henry talked about them. He talks and talks. My head is full of his talking. Mandy. Are you also listening to him? In your darkness? Or aren't you here with me at all? Were my hands too friendly to you? My mother says I have beautiful, slender hands. What will happen to me in Berlin? Who'll be waiting for me? I don't know. But for the first time in my life I know exactly why I'm heading somewhere.

I reach for my pants lying on the floor, pull them over to me, and fish my cell phone out of the pocket. I turn it on, and the display flashes up green. The mailbox voice says: "You have eight new messages. Message playback: first message, received . . ."

I turn off the phone and put it back in my pocket.

Henry's voice: "I took the metro back home. It felt fucking great: my pants were full of shit, I stank of shit all over, and I sat there, my eyes wide open, and kept looking everywhere for Jens. Nobody was at my place. What a relief! I went straight to the bathroom, took off my dirty clothes, and threw them in the sink. Then I got into the tub. As I lay there I kept staring at my shower gel, my shampoo, my towel hanging on the rack, my bathrobe hanging on the rack. Everything was there. And I was lying in the water, and wasn't dead. Suddenly the doorbell rang. Right away it rang a second time. I turned ice-cold in the warm water. I got out of the bathtub and tiptoed with wet feet and bated breath into the living room, to the window. I looked down into the street. His Citroën was there. The doorbell rang three more times, and then quite a while passed before the Citroën drove off. I had to sit down. Thoughts whipped through my brain. What should I do? I thought of my father, who was in some fucking town or other and who I could never reach. I'd have liked to talk to him. Not to my mother. My mom runs around in a panic even when nothing's going on. Can you imagine me telling her about what had happened that day? I had to get out of there. That was my only clear thought. I had no doubt that soon enough I'd find him waiting for me downstairs. Or outside my door. It was getting dark. He'll wait till the lights go on up here. Or till my mother comes back from the bookstore and says: 'Hi there, Jens. Come on in.' He'd drag me back to his car. Shall we go plowing into a truck? Shall we play ghost drivers on the autobahn? Shall we? I got up and suddenly knew what I had to do. I had to get on the first train to Berlin. Because there's someone there I can stay with. A friend of my mother's. She's got a flower store. And this big old apartment. He won't come looking for me in Berlin. Maybe I'll stay there for a while. Maybe forever. As it is, there's nothing to keep me in Munich. Nothing at all. I took a piece of paper and wrote my mother a note: 'I've got to go away for a couple of days, I'll call you, Henry.' I needed some money. There'd been a few envelopes among my Christmas presents. From my grand-parents, my father, various aunts. There'd been money in them. They were still in my desk drawer in my room. I took out the bills—they came to exactly eight hundred and fifty marks. I threw a few things into my backpack. I called a cab. Went down the dark stairwell. I was afraid he'd be back again. Jens, I mean. But the street was empty. A few snowflakes were falling into the lantern light. The cab pulled up." Henry hesitates. "Well, and then I got on this train," he says, and adds: "I like traveling on trains, you know. But this is no joyride for me."

"For me neither, I guess."

"You know the book *Jacob the Liar* by Jurek Becker?" he asks. "It's a great book. You remember the last line? 'We are heading for wherever we are heading.'"

"Yes," I reply, "we are heading for wherever we are heading."

My mouth is totally dry.

We sleep a little. As best we can. Till there's a knock at the door. The voice of the conductor comes from outside: "Forty minutes to Berlin-Wannsee. Breakfast is being served in the dining car."

I open the door a crack and say, "Thanks, we'll head over there."

Henry asks: "Should I go get breakfast, or do you want to?"

"I need to stretch my legs a little," I tell him. "What should I get you?"

"A croissant and some coffee," he says.

I slip into my jeans. As I open the door, Henry says: "Paul." I stop. "Did I bore you with my story?" he asks.

"No, don't worry about it," I say without turning around. "What did you say you wanted? A croissant?"

"Yeah."

I leave the compartment and walk along the empty, narrow, lurching corridor toward the dining car. I find it hard to keep my balance, and I steady myself against the walls. I feel sick. I listened to his story the whole time. But I couldn't get rid of those images inside my head. The images that have been torturing me since I left Berlin four days ago. I've tried to turn them off. But I can't. Mandy. Mandy's face. Her beautiful face. How she looked as she lay there. On the bed. Before I left her. Her face was white. And her eyes were totally white too. And I left her lying there.

I get to the dining car. I tell the woman behind the counter: "One croissant, one salami sandwich, and two coffees." She hands me a tray and I make my way back to the compartment with it. It's even harder now to keep my balance without spilling the coffee. Halfway there I burn my fingers.

Mandy. I met her at Bel Ami, the most elegant brothel in Berlin. Which I wouldn't have been able to afford. But this rich guy took me there. I met him at this titty bar near Stuttgarter Platz. An old guy in a black suit and tie. "Let's go someplace else," he told me. "I'll take you to where they show some real stuff. A true paradise. Don't worry, it'll be my treat."

We went by cab. The "true paradise" was a white villa in Charlottenburg, brightly lit. Admiralstrasse 14. A doorman let us in—a small, short-haired man, also in a black suit and tie. I had the feeling I was entering a golden palace. Red sofas and arm-chairs, enormous golden mirrors, a golden bar, flickering golden candlelight. But what was truly shining was the girls—sitting, standing, sweeping through the room like they were walking on air. They were all in lingerie. I'd never seen anything like it. So much beauty in one place. I thought I'd go crazy. I'm staying here forever, I said to myself. The guy who had taken me there—his name was Frank—laughed and slapped me on the back. "I told you, this place is fucking-A."

We sat down in a corner, and I stared every which way. Suddenly I didn't care about anything. I didn't care that I was sitting in some villa that was fucking incredible. With an old guy I didn't know. I didn't care that I didn't feel at home anywhere, anywhere at all. All that was so far away now. *So far away.* All I wanted was to be with a girl like one of these.

A group of them came over to our table and asked if they could join us.

"Sure thing," Frank said.

He ordered two bottles of champagne, Veuve Clicquot. The girls told us their names and sat down. The bar woman came and filled everyone's glasses.

"What shall we drink to?" Frank asked.

"Let's drink to the night," one of the girls said.

"Okay then, here's to the night!"

We all raised our glasses. Mandy was sitting across from me. Her hair was long and brown, and her eyes were like forget-me-nots. She had very thin eyebrows. She was wearing a black bra, a thong, and black fishnet stockings. I couldn't stop staring at her. At the shadowy line between her breasts, her delicate collarbones, and her graceful, slender neck. Her skin shone all over as if it had been rubbed with oil. I desperately wanted to touch her collarbone. Do nothing but touch her collarbone for the rest of my life.

"You look so sad," Mandy said to me suddenly.

"What?"

"I said, you look sad. Are you sad?" There was a soft shimmer in her eyes.

"Well," I began, "I—"

"But you're so young," a redhead sitting to my left cut in. "You can't be unhappy at your age. You haven't experienced anything yet, even though you might think you have. You don't know what problems are. The problems you think you have aren't problems at all. They're all little, unimportant things." She giggled and drank a sip of champagne.

"I didn't come here with this kid so you could discuss his problems with him," Frank said, laughing. "Today we have no problems. Today we're riding high. What do you say to that, Paul?"

"Sure," I replied.

"Mandy," he said.

"Yes?"

"How are we doing today?"

"You're riding high."

"You said it!"

He turned to another girl, who was already pretty wasted. She was studying her champagne glass from every side. She held it up and looked at it from beneath with wide eyes.

"Vivien, how are you doing today?" Frank asked.

"I'm riding high," she drawled. Frank laughed. Mandy leaned forward. She opened her legs and pressed her palms between them on the chair. Her breasts were squeezed together. I got a hard-on. It pushed up against my jeans. She was hot. I looked at her and imagined her as my girlfriend. Our glances met. Her eyes sparkled.

"You're so young," she said. "Young guys don't usually come here. Hardly ever." She sipped at her champagne and put the glass down carefully on the table. Her tongue slid over her lips. That is my girlfriend, I thought. Mandy. She'll be with me forever. Forever. When we're together, darkness will never threaten me again. I wanted to fuck her then and there. To fuck her till there was nothing left to fuck. And there was nothing to stop me. That's what I was there for. But it all felt sort of weird. Because I wanted to be with her for more than just one night. Mandy, my Mandy.

"I'm sad sometimes too, you know," she said, "but never for long."

"How come?" I asked. "What do you do to cheer up?"

"I stand in front of the mirror and put on some makeup. You should try it too." A hushed smile flitted over her face.

"Great suggestion. I'll give it a try someday."

"How are we doing?" Frank suddenly shouted gleefully. "Hey, Paul? How're we doing?"

"We're riding high."

He asked Vivien how she was doing. She was already all over him. She told him she was riding high and began laughing loudly.

"Do you think some force will come rescue us someday and take us away from earth?" I asked Mandy. "To another place, where we'll never have to be scared anymore? Where we might get to fig-

ure out who we are? Where we can accept ourselves? Where it's warm?"

Mandy didn't answer. Then she said: "You have
such small ears. Such small, delicate ears."

Then she looked at me with her light-drenched
eyes. Let's be together, I thought. Let's be together
forever. We sat there for quite a while. Then Frank
grabbed hold of Vivien and another girl, and said:
"Let's go for it! Come on, Paul!"

Mandy took me by the hand. The five of us went
to the room with the swimming pool. It was enormous. And next to it an enormous water bed.
Dimmed lights, only a shimmering blue rising
from the pool.

"How long do you want us for?" the girls asked.

"Two hours," Frank replied.

The bar woman brought champagne and filled
our glasses. We all undressed as if by a silent com-
mand. My heart almost stopped when Mandy
reached behind her back and unhooked her bra.
The other two girls jumped onto the water bed.
They rolled onto their backs. One of them looked
down and warily eyed one of her breasts.

"Come on over here, we're waiting," Vivien
crooned. Frank joined them. I stared at Mandy.

She looked incredible. Her whole body glittered like a crystal. I stared at her breasts, caressed by the tips of her hair; at her slender waist, her navel, her dark pubic hair. It was shaved to an arrow. I didn't know what to do. Just stand there with my hard-on? I was glad she pulled me into the water. She dove under. Came up again. Water streamed from her hair. She shook her head, rubbed her eyes. Pulled her shoulders back, her breasts jutting forward. Pearls of water were dancing on her skin. I grew dizzy. I wanted to turn into water and cling to her body. The bar woman had put two glasses of champagne on the edge of the pool. We raised them to each other.

"You're so sweet," she said. She took the glass from my hand and put it back down with her glass on the edge of the pool. Then she pressed herself onto me. I almost came. I was shivering. I slowly ran my finger over her navel. Her skin felt really soft in the water, and I gazed at the rippling turquoise. Everything was suddenly turquoise. Mandy said, "Now you will be rescued. Just like you said earlier. You will be rescued by a water princess, who will take you to a place where it is warm. Real warm. And wet."

She dipped under and pressed her lips against my chest. She came up again. With one hand she started working my dick. For a second I lost my balance. I slipped and almost went under. She rubbed my dick faster and faster, all the while looking at me with a smile. My body was writhing. Heat whipped through it. I let my head sink back into the water. She stopped rubbing. She whirled around in the water and pressed her ass against my dick. She took my hands and led them to her tits. I almost died. It felt so fucking great. Mandy leaned back. Her ass kept moving and moving. I kissed her shoulder. Licked away a few water drops. Her skin smelled lightly of chlorine. I peered over her shoulder so I could see her breasts. I pressed them together. She moved away and slowly swam to the steps leading out of the pool. I followed her. She pushed me back onto the steps and sat on me. She reached down and grabbed my dick. I felt myself penetrating her. Her hips pulsated. I felt great. I love you, I thought, I love you like crazy.

Right before I came, she raised herself up, and I felt her hand on my dick again. My whole body jolted and I shot my load. My cum streamed into the water in a white trail. As if a fish had spawned.

A real treat for the guy who'd be in the swimming pool after us. But I didn't care.

This image of me and her in the blue, iridescent water. Her wet hair. Her face. Her breasts floating above the water. This image that I always, always, always have in my head. Now too, as I make my way staggering through the corridor of the railway car with this stupid tray, trying not to spill the coffee. I push the door handle of our compartment down with my elbow.

"At last, some coffee!" Henry calls out enthusiastically.

We're sitting together on my bunk, eating and drinking. We've clapped the top bunk shut. Beyond the window it is still dark. Neither of us says anything. Suddenly Henry asks: "Will we meet up sometime in Berlin?"

"I don't think so," I answer, unable to look him in the eye. There's an uncomfortable silence. It lasts a long time. Finally he asks me something else: "Are you crazy about some girl too?"

"Yeah."

"What's she like?" he asks.

I hesitate.

"Her name's Mandy," I say. The loudspeaker announces: "We will be arriving shortly in Berlin-Wannsee."

I had no idea what the price was for the two hours in Bel Ami. Frank had paid by credit card at the bar. He offered to drop me off at my place, but I told him I'd rather walk. It's about two hours on foot from Bel Ami to my place. But I wanted to be alone. I wanted to think about her undisturbed. How great she was. It was cold, but I didn't feel it. For the first time I actually enjoyed walking the streets. A splinter of moon shone in the sky.

I went back the following day. I told the doorman I was a friend of Frank's, and he let me in right away. Inside, everything was exactly as it had been the day before. The same golden glitter. The same amazing women. But there were more customers. All kinds of guys were walking around, lounging in armchairs, hanging out at the bar. Almost all of them were old and in suits. Smoking, drinking, acting up. I stood in the middle of the room, looking for Mandy. I couldn't see her anywhere. Vivien came up to me. She was wearing a long black see-through gown.

"Hi," she said.

"I'm here for Mandy," I said.

"Um, she's over there."

Now I saw her. She was sitting on a guy's lap, drinking champagne. The guy looked quite good. Mandy was wearing a light blue thong and a matching bra. I sat down on a chair and waited. I saw the guy feeling her up. At some point the two of them went upstairs to the second floor. Vivien came and sat down next to me.

"You want to go with me?"

"No."

A girl came staggering down from the second floor, exchanged a few words with Vivien, and left. Vivien said to me: "She's just spent six hours with a guy up there. Six hours of guzzling champagne. She's had it."

Mandy and the guy took forever to come back down. All the customers had already gone. The girls too. I was the only one left, a glass of wine in front of me. The bar woman and the doorman too. He was sitting in a chair nearby, leafing through a magazine and exchanging a word or two with the bar woman. Mandy followed the guy unsteadily to the bar. He paid, said good-bye, and left. Then she turned around and came to me. I jumped up right away.

"Mandy," I said, "I—"

"I saw you," she said. Her eyes were totally drunk. "Why didn't you go upstairs with another girl? Didn't you see I was busy? Don't tell me you want to go up now."

"I just want to talk to you," I said.

"Well, I'm finished for today," she said. "I have to go to bed—and so do those two." She pointed at the bar woman and the doorman. She hesitated. Then she asked: "What is it you want from me?"

"Please, Mandy," I said. "I need to talk to you. Right now. But not here. Let's go somewhere else. Just for a few moments. Let's go outside. Please."

"Okay," she said. "If I have to."

She told the other two she'd be right back. She slipped into a glittering crimson coat and tied the belt, but in a way that you could still see a lot of skin. Her breasts and bra too. Swaying, she made her way back to the bar, got herself a cigarette and some matches. Then we went outside, in front of the door. It was freezing out there. Snow was falling. Mandy tried to light her cigarette behind her cupped hand. It took awhile. She drew at the cigarette and blew the smoke high into the air. I stood in front of her, at first only able to stare at her. How she stood there in her high heels on the snow-powdered ground. Her long legs, barely covered by the coat, began to shiver. She hugged her torso with both arms, and relaxed barely noticeably as she took a drag from her cigarette.

"I love you," I said. The breath from my mouth was visible. "And I want to be with you. Forever."

"What?"

"I said, I love you. You're the most wonderful being I have ever met. I'm surrounded by night but you make me shine just as you do. And not only now—forever. We belong together. I'll do everything for you. And you won't come to this fucking Bel Ami place anymore. You'll be with me. There'll be no night. Never again."

She looked at me dumbfounded.

"What're you talking about?" she said. "It's fucking cold, and I'm standing here freezing my ass off while you're talking bullshit. I have no intention of being with you. Ever. I'll tell you what I expect of life. Do you know what kind of guys come to Bel

Ami? Important men, rich men, stars, politicians, artists, movie people, musicians, managers. That singer from Southern Comfort always comes here when he's in Germany. He's into me. He's even taken me to concerts, you know what I mean? That's the kind of guy I want to be with—somebody important with loads of cash. Who can offer me the kind of lifestyle I want. That's what I'm waiting for. And hundreds of guys like that come here. One of *them* is going to take me away from this place, not you. I bet you're living off the six hundred marks Daddy sends you every month. What are you, anyway? A student or something?"

She went back inside, and said over her shoulder, "And by the way, I like it here."

I spent Christmas Eve in my apartment. With my roommate Randall. Christmas Day too. We put candles everywhere. We hung out, drank. Talked a little. Mostly we didn't, though.

New Year's Eve. Everyone was going on about the euro. Some people were even wearing euro costumes. It was crazy out on the streets. Premature fireworks went whistling and banging up the house walls. I felt I'd get shot if I didn't run fast enough. When I got to Bel Ami, around ten, the doorman let me in again. Garlands hung from the ceiling, balloons, streamers. There were trays with glasses of champagne everywhere. The girls were walking around like glittering Christmas trees. Mandy sat on a sofa with a few customers and some other girls. She was wearing a golden outfit. She looked beautiful. High spirits, champagne, giggling, groping. I walked up to the group.

"What do you want?" she asked me.

"Can I have a word with you? Just a quick word."

She took her neighbor's hand off her thigh and said, "Sure." She told the others at the table she'd be right back.

She led the way up the stairs to the second floor. She was wearing her hair pinned up. I gazed the whole time at her slender neck. She opened the door to one of the rooms. We went inside. She sat down on the bed and crossed her legs.

"Well?" she said.

Ten minutes later I went back down the stairs. Walked through the room where all the people were sitting and laughing, and took a glass of champagne. I walked past the doorman, out into the street. Far away, I heard the popping of fireworks and all the other stuff. I walked a few paces down the street, stopped, and drank the champagne in a single gulp. Then I threw the glass into the street. It was New Year's Eve.

The next morning I took the train to Munich, to my parents. I no longer had my room there—they were using it for other things—so I slept in my mother's study. And there were the slices of kiwi at night.

"Paul?" Henry says. "Why can't we meet up in Berlin? Is it because you don't like me?"

"It's got nothing to do with you," I answer. I hesitate. "I ran away from something. But I can't run anymore. I just can't."

"Are you sure we can't get together?" Henry says. "I mean, it would be cool to go to the movies or something. Or just hang and talk. We could be friends."

"No."

He is silent, and then asks: "Is it because of the story I told you?"

I shake my head.

"Oh well," he says. "Whatever. But I just want you to know that I won't be forgetting this train ride anytime soon. For me it was the weirdest train ride ever. You can bet I'll be telling people about it forever. I'm glad you ended up in this compartment. That I got to know you."

"Thanks," I say. "I won't be forgetting this train ride anytime soon, either." And after a while I add: "Take good care of yourself."

We smile at each other. The voice on the loudspeaker says: "The train is approaching Berlin–Zoologischer Garten."

Henry and I take our bags and go out into the corridor. The lights of the dark city are steeped in sleep. The girl who had fallen down in the corridor the night before is also there with her friend. I smile at one of them—she smiles back.

We stand there silently. There's only the sound of the train, which is now slowing down.

"So, here we are in Berlin," Henry says quietly.

"Yeah, here we are in Berlin," I repeat.

The train pulls into the station. "Hey, there's the Kaiser Wilhelm Memorial Church!" he shouts excitedly, pointing out the window. The train stops, its wheels grinding. I feel the strap of my bag pressing into my shoulder. We get off. It's mild out. The air smells of train station. Shouting. People hugging one another. The sound of roller bags being pulled along the platform. Henry next to me. Two men step out from the crowd. Right in front, by the tracks. They approach us. One is wearing a brown parka, the other a gray coat. One of them holds out his badge.

"Are you Paul Wielandt?" he asks me.

"Yes."

"You are under arrest on suspicion of having murdered the prostitute Luise Sheffler."

Henry stares at me, thunderstruck. His jaw drops. There's a giant question mark on his face. He hasn't yet strapped on his backpack. He lets it fall on the platform. As the two men lead me off, I turn around to look at him. One of the men grabs me by the shoulder.

"Okay, okay!" I say. "I just want to tell that guy something." He lets go. But he and his colleague stay close to me. I walk back to Henry. He looks at me.

"I guess I'm just not a storyteller like you," I say.

ALSO BY BENJAMIN LEBERT

*"Anything he writes is, by definition, pitch-perfect."*
—The New York Times Book Review

CRAZY

When we meet sixteen-year-old Benni, he's entering the fifth boarding school of his short academic career. He's been kicked out of the other four. Paralyzed on his left side and a veteran failure at certain subjects, Benni doesn't have much hope that he'll make it at this new school. But all that changes when he meets his roommate, Janosch, and the motley band of friends that follow him everywhere. Together, Benni and his pals are in a hurry to figure out the world of girls, booze, sex, philosophy, literature, music, and anything else they can think of. Their needs take them everywhere—the local sex clinic, the girls' dorm, city strip clubs—as Benni lets us in on "the crazy life" that he figures is the only way to deal with the crazy world and who he is. Benjamin Lebert delivers an exhilarating picture of the time in life when everyone feels a little unstrung but wants to know, do, be everything at once—whatever.

Fiction/978-1-4000-7707-6

THE BLACK BOOK
by Orhan Pamuk

Galip is a lawyer living in Istanbul. His wife, Rüya, has disappeared. Could she have left him for her ex-husband or Celâl, a popular newspaper columnist? But Celâl, too, seems to have vanished. As Galip investigates, he finds himself assuming the enviable Celâl's identity, wearing his clothes, answering his phone calls, even writing his columns. Galip pursues every conceivable clue, and when he receives a death threat, he begins to fear the worst. *The Black Book* is the cherished Turkish cult novel in which Orhan Pamuk found his original voice, and now, in this beautiful new translation, English-language readers, too, may encounter all its riches.

Fiction/Literature/978-1-4000-7865-3

DONA FLOR AND HER TWO HUSBANDS
by Jorge Amado

It surprises no one that the charming but wayward Vadinho dos Guimaraes—a gambler notorious for never winning—dies during Carnival. His long-suffering widow Dona Flor devotes herself to her cooking school and her friends, who urge her to remarry. She is soon drawn to a kind pharmacist who is everything Vadinho was not, and is happy to marry him. But after her wedding she finds herself dreaming about her first husband's amorous attentions; and one evening Vadinho himself appears by her bed to claim his marital rights.

Fiction/Literature/978-0-307-27664-3

HERE IS WHERE WE MEET
by John Berger

John Berger returns us to the captivating play and narrative allure of his previous novels with a shimmering fiction drawn from chapters of his own life. One hot afternoon in Lisbon, the narrator finds his long-dead mother seated on a park bench. "The dead don't stay where they are buried," she tells him. And so begins a remarkable odyssey, told in simple yet gorgeous prose, that carries us from the London Blitz in 1943 to a Polish market, to a Paleolithic cave, to the Ritz Hotel in Madrid without losing its foothold in the sensuous present.

Fiction/Literature/978-1-4000-7933-9

## ISTANBUL
### *Memories and the City*
### by Orhan Pamuk

Orhan Pamuk was born in Istanbul and still lives in the family apartment building where his mother first held him in her arms. His portrait of his city is thus also a self-portrait, refracted by memory and the melancholy—or *hüzün*—that all *Istanbullus* share: the sadness that comes of living amid the ruins of a lost empire. With cinematic fluidity, Pamuk moves from his glamorous, unhappy parents to the gorgeous, decrepit mansions overlooking the Bosphorus; from the dawning of his self-consciousness to the writers and painters—both Turkish and foreign—who would shape his consciousness of his city. Like Joyce's Dublin and Borges's Buenos Aires, *Istanbul* is a triumphant encounter of place and sensibility, beautifully written and immensely moving.

Memoir/978-1-4000-3388-1


## THE MAGIC KEYS
### by Albert Murray

*The Magic Keys* winningly evokes the coming to maturity and the joyful rhythms of youth of one of the great characters in contemporary American literature: Alabama-born Scooter, the central protagonist of Albert Murray's highly acclaimed novels *Train Whistle Guitar*, *The Spyglass Tree*, and *The Seven League Boots*.

Fiction/Literature/978-0-375-42353-6


## MAPS FOR LOST LOVERS
### by Nadeem Aslam

Jugnu and Chanda have disappeared. Like thousands of people all over England, they were lovers and living together out of wedlock. To Chanda's family, however, the disgrace was unforgivable—perhaps enough to warrant murder. As he explores the disappearance and its aftermath through the eyes of Jugnu's worldly older brother, Shamas, and his devout wife, Kaukab, Nadeem Aslam creates a closely observed and affecting portrait of people whose traditions threaten to bury them alive. The result is intimate, affecting, tragic and suspenseful.

Fiction/Literature/978-1-4000-7697-0

## NO COUNTRY FOR OLD MEN
### by Cormac McCarthy

In his blistering new novel, Cormac McCarthy returns to the Texas–Mexico border, the setting of his famed Border Trilogy. The time is our own, when rustlers have given way to drug-runners and small towns have become free-fire zones. A good old boy named Llewellyn Moss finds a pickup truck surrounded by dead men. A load of heroin and two million dollars in cash are still in the back. When Moss takes the money, he sets off a chain reaction of catastrophic violence that not even the law can contain. Encompassing themes as ancient as the Bible and as bloodily contemporary as this morning's headlines, *No Country for Old Men* is a triumph.

Fiction/Literature/978-0-375-70667-7

## THE SEA
### by John Banville

In this luminous novel about love, loss, and the unpredictable power of memory, John Banville introduces us to Max Morden, a middle-aged Irishman who has gone back to the seaside town where he spent his summer holidays as a child to cope with the recent loss of his wife. It is also a return to the place where he met the Graces, the well-heeled family with whom he experienced the strange suddenness of both love and death for the first time. What Max comes to understand about the past, and about its indelible effects on him, is at the center of this elegiac, gorgeously written novel—among the finest we have had from this masterful writer.

Fiction/Literature/978-1-4000-9702-9